The Pure Heart

Don't you love the wildness of the Scottish borderlands? Every now and then, travelling through this dramatic and historic landscape, you glimpse a ruin on a lonely hillside that's crying out to tell you its story . . . but I doubt any of these could be as strange, haunting and gripping as Trudi Tweedie's twisted debut. The winner of the Times/Chicken House Children's Fiction Competition, Trudi is a rare talent – and this tale is as unusual as it is chilling. Prepare to be swept away.

BARRY CUNNINGHAM
Publisher
Chicken House

PS There's a useful glossary on page 269.

The Pure Heart

TRUDI TWEEDIE

Chicken House

2 PALMER STREET, FROME, SOMERSET BA11 1DS

First published in Great Britain in 2020
Chicken House
2 Palmer Street
Frome, Somerset BA11 1DS
United Kingdom
www.chickenhousebooks.com

Cover and interior design by Steve Wells
Cover illustration by Jeff Fisher
Typeset by Dorchester Typesetting Group Ltd
Printed and bound in Great Britain by CPI Group (UK) Ltd, Croydon CR0 4YY

The paper used in this Chicken House book is made
from wood grown in sustainable forests.

1 3 5 7 9 10 8 6 4 2

British Library Cataloguing in Publication data available.

PB ISBN 978-1-912626-00-7
eISBN 978-1-912626-73-1

To Andy, Fara and Innes

I t was early evening, mid-September when the boat
came to the bay.

The craft cut effortlessly through the storm-crested
waves, their tips crowned orange by the evening sun.

Down below on the shore the men gathered like
swarming ants, whilst we girls watched from outside our
stone cottages, readily distracted from plucking the last
rabble of summer puffins. Artair was down there too,
part of the huddle of island men who had mustered in the
shallows ready to take the measure of the sailor.

But although they all wore the same black shirts and
tam-o'-shanters, Artair stood out like a beacon to me, for
not only would he one day be chief of these islands, but

by the next full moon I would be his wife.

The women had all but stopped plucking by now, abandoning half-bald birds to stand out on the ridge where they cooed at the spectacle of dazzling crimson sails, puffed up tight as pillows with Atlantic squall. An older woman shouted above the wind that the boat was far too small for a seafaring vessel, yet there it was, buoying along keenly, its narrow bow cleaving apart the steely waters like a sharp blade through cooked flesh.

At the helm, a solitary figure made to drop anchor.

'Look, *Iseabail*!' said my younger sister Eilidh, securing her puffin with a stone and rushing to join the others. 'A sailor has captained his craft alone, right through that terrible storm.'

'I wonder where he has come from,' I said, transfixed by the sight of the stranger, dressed in a pale flotilla of clothes. He alighted alone from his craft to be greeted by our men. There was sight of no other aboard.

'Let's go down and see,' said Eilidh, wiping her hands on her apron.

'We mustn't,' I protested, trying to hide my excitement at the sight of the man who had single-handedly made it to our barren glut of rocks. Fifty miles west of the Outer Hebrides, one hundred from the Scottish mainland, a trip from even our closest neighbours took several days of hard sail and oar. Few would risk their lives in the summer months to come here, only the reckless once the autumn storms had begun.

'What harm to us all can one man be?' protested my sister, making to join the other women.

But I held on to her arm tightly. At seventeen, I was two years older than her. It was expected of me.

'He might bring disease,' I said, trying to dissuade her although the man looked healthy enough. He was now on the shore, shaking the hands of the elders, the sheep-dogs circling him joyously. Meanwhile all the other women and girls had abandoned their posts and were starting to make their way down the slope from the stone cottages, though none dared venture as far as the shore.

'What's going on, Iseabail?' said Mammy, coming out through the open blackhouse door, a cloud of fishy stew in her wake.

'A stranger, Mammy,' I said, without letting the thrill seep into my voice.

'Came in a boat all by himself,' added Eilidh, struggling to free herself from my grip.

'Let the men deal with him,' snapped Mammy, hold-ing open the door. 'And both of you come inside!'

Eilidh was furious. She twisted free before pushing under the thatch into the windowless cottage. 'You're such a goody-goody!' she spat at me.

'You were right to stop her,' said Mammy as we too went inside. 'We will know soon enough what all that is about.'

A short while later, there was a rap at the door and I knew from the rhythm just who it would be.

Mammy pulled back the door. 'Ah, Artair,' she said cagily. 'What news do you bring?'

'We need to borrow Iseabail,' he said, a quickness of breath disguising his apprehension of my mother. He shot me a glance over the top of Mammy's head, enough to cause my tummy to ripple.

I dipped my head, knowing that my cheeks had coloured up.

'What on earth for?' asked Mammy sharply, blocking Eilidh from escaping through the open door with her elbow.

'The man . . . the sailor . . . he brings a letter, but none of us have enough words to read it,' said Artair unsteadily.

'Well, we want nothing to do with him or his letter!' said Mammy. 'Tell the men that they'll have to do without her. Can't this stranger read it out for them?' And with this she slammed the door shut, plunging us three McCleod women back into dimness.

I sat by the hearth, the flames illuminating my face. 'I don't mind going,' I said piously, hiding my exhilaration at the prospect of reading the letter. As always, I hungered for news of the outside world – and for any opportunity to breach the fraternity of the men's council. 'I'm sure it won't take long . . . as long as it's written in Gaelic.'

It wasn't the first time I'd been called upon for such a duty. Since Father had died, I was the one the men sought out to read any communication from the outside world – although the men who bore these messages had never been strangers before.

'If she's going, so am I!' said Eilidh indignantly.

'Neither of you are going!' said Mammy. 'That sailor is probably riddled with all manner of nasty things.' She returned to her stew, poking the fire so sharply that a crest of sparks shot up. 'God knows why you taught Iseabail to read, Dougal,' she muttered under her breath, like Father was still around, standing by her side at the hearth. 'And you were daft enough to make no secret of it!'

'That's the only reason Artair wants to marry Iseabail,' said Eilidh, folding her arms over her bosom in a sulk. 'Because she can read. But I bet he thinks I'm far prettier.'

I didn't take the bait, instead finding comfort by stroking the scar on my left wrist. It marked where Eilidh had stabbed me with a sharp piece of animal bone, the day that Artair asked Mammy for my hand in marriage. Artair was the finest young man that our island had to offer and Eilidh, despite only being fifteen, had fancied that he might ask her instead.

The morning after I accepted his proposal, Artair followed island tradition by balancing on the Maiden's Rock, a precarious cliff ledge dangling high over the crashing waves of the Atlantic, to prove he would make a worthy husband. To prove his love for me – and only me.

'Father tried to teach you to read,' I said calmly. Eilidh was such a jealous girl that I had to let most of what flew out of her mouth wash over me. 'But you were too impatient to sit, remember?'

'Sitting is boring,' she replied, twirling a coil of luxuriant dark hair around her finger. But it sounded so ridiculous that we both burst into fits of laughter. I was glad our arguments, although often heated, were always short-lived.

'Well, don't worry, you'll have a second chance,' I said, as our giggles faded. 'I intend to make sure everyone is taught their letters when Artair becomes chief. We've already discussed it – it will be a good thing for the island.'

'Over my dead body,' said Mammy, turning to wield the poker. 'I had to swallow my tongue every night when your father got those infernal books out! But you . . . you couldn't get enough of them!'

'Pity we don't still have them,' I mumbled. For after Father was swept out to sea, grief had driven Mammy into snapping all the writing slates, throwing every single one of his books on to the pyre.

'I heard that,' Mammy battered on. 'Now not another word on the matter – or I'll slap the beaks off the both of you, so I will.'

Eilidh and I stole a glance at one another through the peaty smoke. Both of us were trying our best not to break out in giggles again.

But then there was another knock at the door. Different this time, more authoritative.

Innes Ferguson, Artair's father and chief of the islands of St Kilda, stood at the door.

'Iseabail,' he said calmly, looking past my mother like she didn't exist. 'You will come with me now.'

The sailor had been led up to the chief's cottage and was now being offered gannet soup to be taken on the bench outside of my future father-in-law's house. But Innes stopped me several yards short of where the men crowded there – a blatant reminder that I was not their equal. Instead he signalled for Artair to bring the letter whilst I took a seat on a nearby rock. Mammy, who had insisted on accompanying me, stood just off to the side, still holding Eilidh's arm tightly.

'The sailor says he's just the messenger,' said Innes. The chief's voice was calm but flecked with trepidation as he watched his son retreat, leaving us four alone. 'Says he was sent to deliver this to the chief of these islands. But claims he can't read a word himself. Speaks Gaelic in a funny way too.'

'Is it an English accent he has . . . or maybe Irish?' I enquired, accepting the scroll of parchment from the chief's hands. 'Scandinavian?'

'Never you mind,' said Innes, which meant that he couldn't work out where the man might be from. 'Just tell me what it says . . . and be quick about it!'

The seal on the parchment had been broken, its red

wax counter now separated clumsily in two halves with the opening flapping in the wind.

I pressed it back together. 'It's a lion,' I observed as the head and body were once more united. 'What country is that from?'

But the chief was impatient. 'Get on with it, girl!' He glowered.

'Please, Iseabail.' Mammy bent to whisper in my ear, mortified at my boldness. 'Just do as the chief asks.'

I unrolled the scroll of parchment, hands shaking as the beauty of the manuscript unfolded on to my lap; I had never seen anything like it before. Unable to contain herself any more, Eilidh peered over my shoulder, a gasp escaping her plump lips.

My eyes darted greedily up and down the parchment as I held it open against the wind, wondering where to begin. It was written in Gaelic – the main body etched out beautifully in black calligraphy, the first character of each paragraph enlarged and woven into twisted Celtic bands. But I was distracted by the decorated margins which snaked with vines and serpent-like creatures, inked solid with colours that I didn't even have a name for.

I tried to settle my gaze, but the writing was so full of flicks and wisps that it was several moments before I could decipher anything it said.

'At least tell me who it is from?' said Innes, prodding me in the back sharply.

'Let's see,' I said, though for a minute I'd completely

forgotten he was standing there. Forgotten that all three of them were standing behind me, waiting for me to say something. My eyes scrolled down to the signature at the bottom.

'Plaustrell,' I said finally, looking up at the chief's anxious face. 'This letter is from a man named Alexander Plaustrell.'

Innes's frown deepened at the mention of the strange name. 'What does it say? What does this Plaustrell person want?'

The light was fading as the sun slid behind the sea stacks, dipping the islands into blue-blackness – but I held the letter up to the dying light and read the first paragraphs aloud.

The letter, addressed boldly to the chief of our islands, began with asking a favour; that favour was for the loan of a girl.

Innes Ferguson looked perplexed at the request. 'Why would I give up one of my girls to this . . . what does he say he is again? A merchant?'

'That's what he claims here,' I said, pointing to the relevant part of the text I'd already read out. 'A merchant of great wealth. Says he lives in a grand house situated in the borderlands between England and Scotland.' I read out more, my voice faltering as I saw the look on Mammy's face.

'And now he wants a girl from here to look after his daughter!' exclaimed Mammy, repeating back what I had just read. 'Just because his wife died of the plague? Well, of all the things!'

'He says that he is looking for a special girl – one from a remote place, untouched by the evils of the outside world,' I progressed.

The phrase that the merchant had used was *caileag ghealchridheach* – a girl that is pure of heart.

'Does this man explain himself further?' Innes responded, standing on his toes to look down to the beach, checking the movements of the sailor.

He did. For the letter went on to say that in return for her services, the chosen girl was promised a luxurious life, full of comfort.

'Anything else?' said Innes, still obviously dissatisfied with what the merchant was offering up in return for a precious girl of childbearing age.

'Yes . . . here it is,' I said, following the lines I had not yet read with my finger. '*A boat will be dispatched to your shores in mid-winter, loaded with grain, candles and timber. A token of my gratitude.*'

A look of contemplation passed over Innes's face. Last winter had been unforgiving and we'd lost several islanders to cold and starvation. Since then, there had been rumblings of dissent, families with talk of moving to the Hebrides for a less brutal life, where men didn't risk their necks gathering seabirds from the treacherous cliffs, where women's new-born children would not perish from the eight-day sickness. A boat of supplies in mid-winter would save lives . . . and strengthen Innes's power.

'Surely this is some kind of trick?' I said, turning nervously to look back up at Innes. 'Whoever heard of a boat making it through here in winter?'

Then again, I thought, whoever heard of a man sailing a ship here on his own?

But Innes just stabbed a broad finger back at the writing. 'That's not for you to decide,' he said roughly, but now he was looking directly at Eilidh. 'Now, what else does it say?'

My finger wound nervously to the last paragraph. '*The chosen girl would be given the choice to return to the islands, if she so wished.*'

But as I spoke these words with some relief, my eyes skipped down to the last line and I froze. What was written there was about to change everything.

The others, assuming that I had finished the letter, stood behind the rock where I sat, brewing it over.

'I'll go,' said Eilidh defiantly, stepping forward and spinning round to face Innes. 'I *want* to go!'

Mother pressed a hand to her own mouth. 'Eilidh, no!' she said between her fingers. 'The chief will not be sending anyone.'

But one look at Innes and we all knew that this was not the case.

'Of course it has to be me,' continued Eilidh, her brown eyes flashing rebelliously. 'Fionna McQueen's father is too powerful, he'll not let her go. Then there's the McKinnon twins – one isn't right in the head, the other too sickly to make the journey.'

'Stop it!' cried Mammy, her voice catching in her throat. But Eilidh was on fire now, her dark chestnut mane whipping in the wind.

'And Iseabail is engaged to Artair. It *has* to be me.'

'That is for the men to decide,' snapped Innes, though he had obviously been thinking the exact same thing as Eilidh. 'Though it would be easier if the chosen girl went willingly.'

Mammy looked at him aghast. She loved both her daughters, but losing her youngest would probably kill her. 'You are to consider this offer?' she cried, incredulous. 'And these supplies, getting through here in the winter – why, it's ludicrous!'

But Innes remained tight-lipped. Mammy looked desperately to me for help. And I gave it to her.

'Don't worry, Mammy, it can't be Eilidh,' I breathed, my voice barely breaking above the noise of the wind.

But Mammy's relief was short-lived.

'Because it says here . . .' I went on, lowering the scroll because my hands were shaking. 'It says that the young lady chosen must be able to read and write.'

That night, I hardly slept a wink, and when I did I dreamt only of the letter. Black calligraphy snaked around my dreams, like demons tempting me into the afterlife. Would this be my last night here, sharing a simple bunk with my sister? Would the men really send me across that churning black ocean all the way to Scotland – all for a thin promise of winter supplies?

I crept out from the curtain which separated the bed from the rest of the blackhouse and lit a tallow from the embers. In his haste to re-join the men, Innes had left the parchment with me and I had sneaked it away in my smock.

The beauty of the scroll was enhanced by the candle-light. I unfurled it, tracing each curling letter with a sooty finger. Who was this mysterious merchant? And why had he gone to such lengths just to find a suitable companion for his daughter? *A girl pure of heart.*

My mind conjured up his grand house filled with fancy rooms, brimming with plush furniture. Maybe it had one of those libraries Father had spoken about – an entire room given over simply to books and reading!

Father had drowned, along with his stories of the outside world, but I still burnt to know of what lay beyond the horizon.

I looked about the blackhouse – just one room containing everything we needed squashed bare stone wall to bare stone wall. And when the winter was bad we had to find room for animals in here too. Would a year spent as companion to a rich, educated girl be such a bad thing? I could return to the island full of knowledge. It would make me a more worthy leader.

I rolled the scroll up carefully and pushed it into a crack in the wall where I kept secret things, slipping out of the blackhouse and heading for the shore.

Only a smattering of clouds scudded across the toenail moon which had risen from behind the incisor-sharp sea stacks. The sky glittered, the stars too numerous to pick out any single one. Would the skies in the borderlands be just as celestial? Would the merchant's daughter be at this moment staring up at the very same moon?

My bare toes navigated down the well-worn path to the beach, the bay opening below me like an apron. The breeze lifted my hair from my shoulders, massaging my cheeks with soft briny fingers as I stole past the litter of blackhouses, all nuzzled close to one another for shelter. The wind was still tepid from summer but it had an edge to it, winter approaching with stealth, circling like a white-tailed eagle.

Light was still spilling from under the door of the largest one belonging to the Fergusons, the faint murmur of men in council mingling with the gentle lap of the waves.

Down below, the boat sat in the bay, its sails lowered, rising and falling on the calm waters, rocking its single occupant to sleep. The sailor would have been fed well, but strangers were rarely invited to spend a night in one of our beds.

I sat down on the sand to be immediately greeted by one of the sheepdogs left on guard duty. This one I called Gaoth because she could run like the wind. I urged the dog to be quiet so as not to raise the men and she obliged by lying submissively on her back, demanding a tickle.

'You are supposed to be working, you naughty thing,' I chided her. 'Guarding us from whoever is aboard that boat.'

I looked out to the boat. That little craft that had come from afar. Maybe it had already sailed around all the edges of the world . . . if indeed the world had edges at all. Father had said that the world was round like a pebble, but Mammy insisted that was nonsense. I wondered if I would now find out for myself.

'Do you think that the men will send me away?' I said to Gaoth, stroking her dutiful head.

The dog let out a soft whimper.

'Innes will surely only do what is best for everyone,' I said, laying my cheek against hers. 'He knows that if I go, I will return to fulfil my duties here.'

But then suddenly the dog sat bolt upright.

'What is it, Gaoth?' I questioned, observing her wet nose pointing out to the bay like she'd caught the scent of something.

The dog whimpered again and moved around me protectively in a circle.

'It's OK,' I reassured her, looking out towards the craft where all seemed to be still. I couldn't make out the figure aboard so assumed the sailor to be lying down, sleeping.

But then I heard it. A guttural noise, like the babbling of nesting fulmars. But that sound belonged to the sea stacks – the birds never roosted down here and most had flown the islands now for the winter.

I listened again, sure it was coming from the bay, holding the dog by her scruff and willing her not to bark.

'Shhh,' I hissed, listening as intently as Gaoth, who was cocking her head to one side to hear better.

There it was again. But sharper this time. Unearthly, almost. It reminded me of, but was not quite, the screech of a herring gull. A frisson of prickles ran down my spine.

'What is that?' I whispered.

Gaoth was unable to contain herself any more. She let out a yap and the strange noise was immediately silenced.

Then the door of Innes's blackhouse clicked open, letting out a beam of yellow light.

I stood and ran. The men would be angry if they found me here. My feet found the sandy path and I sprinted behind a stone cleit, observing the three hefty shadows that emerged and ran down to the shore.

I wove back through the jumble of silent blackhouses, still pondering the strange noise, my fingertips guiding me through their maze of rough-hewn walls.

But someone was following me.

'I knew you wouldn't be in bed,' said a hissed whisper, and Artair emerged from behind a collapsed wall.

Without another word, he pulled me into his arms, my head burrowing into his musky beard.

'You are not with the men?' I whispered as I inhaled him, wondering if he already knew the answer to their debate.

'They sent me away a while back,' he said, a hint of desperation creeping into his voice. 'Said I'm too close to it all to make a rational decision.'

But the tone of his voice revealed everything. The men had decided to send me away.

His tears came quickly, falling warm on to my cheek, mingling with my own.

'I'll wait for you, Iseabail,' he said, swallowing hard to regain control. 'I promise that I will wait for you.'

The knock came early the next morning, just after first light. Innes Ferguson come to convey the decision reached last night. The island elders had voted unanimously to send me away with the sailor.

I myself had only just slipped back into the blackhouse. Artair and I had been up all night, climbing the cliffs, discussing our plans for when I returned. But mostly we had held each other tightly, staring out to the curve of the horizon, to the edge of our world, where the glittering stars morphed into the rippling ocean.

When Innes left, Mammy regarded our sealskin trunk in a daze, trying to work out what an island girl promised all the riches in the world would possibly need to take with her.

'That trunk belonged to Father, didn't it?' I said, trying to lighten the mood though my tummy was rigid with nerves. 'I'll look after it – bring it back in good condition.'

'I don't care if I never see the cursed thing again,' said Mammy, shaking her head at the disbelief of the situation. 'Your father brought it when he returned to marry me, packed with all those books and quills. Look at all the trouble it has caused us.'

Father had been sent by our landlords in the Outer Hebrides to collect rents paid with sheep hides and fish oil. But he'd fallen for Mammy, and in the end he'd settled here instead.

'But Father loved this trunk,' I said, stroking the smooth pelt stretched out over strips of driftwood. 'And he loved you.'

But Mammy just slapped my hand away, quickly packing the trunk as if to get it over with. Dried puffin, rough bread, a spare smock, a black and white hide from the finest Soay sheep, shoes sewn from a pair of gannets and, even more randomly, an animal skull bleached buff-white by sun, salt and sea. I guess in the end she decided that I needed things that would remind me of this place, things that would bring me back one day.

It was Innes who escorted me from the blackhouse, linking my arm firmly as we walked down to the shore. Everyone that I had ever known was waiting for me there, my whole entire world standing on that narrow strip of creamy sand. I had lingered last in the blackhouse, committing every inch of my modest home to memory.

'I give my word that Artair will not be married for one year to the day,' said Innes. 'Please, Iseabail – try and make it back safely before then.'

I nodded my head. Innes Ferguson was famed for being a man of his word and if this merchant was too, then by the time September came again, I would be back on home soil, armed with valuable experience of the outside world. Still, my stomach knotted at the sight of the gathering on the shore, the crowd forming a horse-shoe at the water's edge around the boat.

'I must tell you,' said Innes watchfully, 'we are not sending you just for the promise of supplies.'

'Then why?' I asked, bewildered.

We were near enough to the crowd now to see that most would not meet my gaze. I spotted Artair standing with my sister near to the boat but had lost sight of Mammy.

'For what other reason are you sending me?'

'It's the strange sailor,' began Innes. 'The men are afraid of him.'

What harm to us all can one man be? My sister's words when the boat sailed into the bay came back to haunt me. I stopped and looked up at the chief for an explanation.

'Last night, we heard cries coming from the boat,' he said. 'Noises that were not human.'

'Not human?' I repeated, thinking of the sounds that I could not explain, the ones that had caused Gaoth to circle me protectively. I could not let on that I had heard them too. 'Whatever do you mean?'

'We want the sailor to leave our shores as soon as possible,' said the chief, taking my arm again and urging me on. 'We need to fulfil that letter's request – otherwise more of his kind might come.'

'What do you mean – more of his kind?'

I looked at the sailor sitting at the helm of his boat, ready to man the rudder. I noticed for the first time how willowy he was, especially compared to the squat men of the island. His pale papery clothes stood out, ethereal against the dark sea, giving him the outline of an angel.

'You will see that there is a strange symbol painted on the bow of his boat,' continued Innes seriously. 'An eye of some kind. The men think it might be the sign of the Devil.'

'The Devil?' I said, my voice rising. 'And yet you still send me?' Any excitement I had about leaving had quickly shifted to fear.

'For your mother's sake, please go quietly,' said the chief, taking my arm again. Tighter this time. 'You will see that this is already difficult for her. I'm telling you this to warn you, Iseabail. Be careful. Keep God close to your heart.'

Too soon we reached the shore and the hushed crowd parted for me. I could see Mammy now, being supported by several women.

Innes guided me straight past to where Eilidh and Artair stood up to their knees in the shallows. I could now make out the symbol Innes had spoken of, just behind Artair's head: a single eye painted in black on the bow, a tear curling out from it. What on earth did it mean?

Artair opened his arms and I ran to him sobbing, the fright finally escaping me.

'Remember all that we discussed last night,' said Artair, his strong hands around my waist. 'Just think of all the things that you will learn – all the knowledge you will bring back to the island.'

I turned to look at the boat, my throat as dry as a husk. The eye bobbed in the water but wasn't too frightening up close, the black paint blistered and peeling.

I turned to look back up at Artair, into the deep brown eyes of this young man who I'd known all of my life. The man who was still my destiny. Everything was going to be all right.

Eilidh took my hand and made her way to the boat, looking up at the sailor who sat at the back at the helm. 'Take good care of her,' she said. 'Take good care of my sister.'

The bay was shrouded in mist, which only intensified the presence of my single companion, the shore soon dissolving along with its inhabitants. The sailor glanced across whilst he leant back on the cabin door, steering calmly, his eyes lingering for a moment on my bare toes. I stared back fiercely at his outlandish clothes, his wavy dark hair and too closely cropped beard, but he wouldn't meet my gaze.

I was still half expecting one of the men to come rowing out through the fog, Innes having changed his mind. But in no time at all we were clear of the bay, skirting the sharpness of Stac an Armin.

That's when the sailor sat upright. 'Here, take this,' he

urged, indicating that I should take the rudder. But so taken was I by his strange accent and the way it rang out in the clear, cold air that I didn't move a muscle.

'Please, miss,' he continued, his Gaelic unsure, stilted, his eyes kept downcast. 'The wind has changed, and we could be blown back on to the rocks.'

I stood wobbly on my sea legs, swapping places with him. Then I sat down at the helm, grasping the wooden tiller like it was the head of a poisonous snake.

'Here, let me show you,' he said in an amused tone, settling himself beside me. Then he clamped a slim, suntanned hand over my white knuckles.

I recoiled at the intimacy but said nothing as he explained the basics, how to steer into the choppy waves, in which general direction we were heading and some other things that I didn't quite follow. He spoke patiently, his white blouse flapping like a delicate butterfly against my rough smock, but seemed somehow afraid to look at me directly. Up close his green waistcoat looked imposs-ibly shiny and thin and he smelt sweetly fragrant, like wild thyme mixed with gorse.

But there were no outward signs of any devilishness or that he was anything more or less than human.

'What's that thing painted on the front of the boat?' I blurted out as he slid out again to tend the sails, deter-mined to eradicate what little fear I still had of him.

'It's known as the Eye of Horus,' he replied as I grappled with the rudder. 'A common talisman – used by

sailors to ward off bad weather, that's all. I should introduce myself by the way: my name is Marcus Amanza. At
your service.'

'It's nothing to do with the Devil then?' I pressed on,
finally getting the hang of the steering.

'It's just a little token of protection,' he laughed, a
gathering of crow's feet mustering around his eyes. 'We
sailors are a superstitious lot.'

I wondered about his age. His skin was weathered and
his dark hair showed the first signs of grey. Still, I could
have placed him anywhere between twenty years and forty.

'Will you be kind enough to tell me your name?' he
said from somewhere behind the sails, ducking down
artfully as they swung about, tying a plethora of compli-
cated knots.

'Iseabail,' I replied. 'My name is Iseabail McCleod.'

'Ish-ah-bel,' he said, coming to a standstill as he
melodically sounded out my name. 'Just like the French
Isabelle.'

But I was looking back over my shoulder now. Only
the tops of St Kilda pointed up through the mist, their
crags iced with guano. 'I was to marry the chief's son in
less than a month,' I explained, my mind drawn back to
last night up on the cliffs. 'I was to be a Ferguson – a
McCleod woman no more.'

'Well, I know nothing about that,' said Marcus, squat-
ting to rummage in a sack. 'I was only sent to take a girl to
the mainland.'

He made it sound so trifling. Not like I'd been ripped away from everything that I had ever known.

'Oh, and I was instructed to give this to the chosen girl,' he said, drawing out a flat leather box from the inside of his waistcoat. We swapped seats: I took the box while he took the rudder. 'You are to put it on.'

Balancing it on my knees, I flipped open the lid. Inside sat a necklace of leather twine with a perfectly round white stone wound into the middle, resting on a nest of velvet. The box was finer than the necklace, I thought.

'Go on then,' he said.

'This is a present?' I said, bemused.

'I suppose that it must be,' he said nonchalantly.

I held the stone up by the twine. It was perfectly white but glinted purple, even in the overcast sky.

'It's a sea-pearl,' I observed, looking to Marcus for confirmation. 'We call them moon crystals back at home.'

I didn't want to seem ungrateful but pearls were common on our islands. I myself had acquired several, prised from the disgruntled mouths of mussels and clams. I had hidden them with my other secret things in the crack in the walls of the blackhouse.

'Just put it on,' said Marcus, impatient now.

'What strange requests this merchant has,' I said, stringing it round my neck and tying the cord. Marcus's eyes followed the pearl as it came to rest on my bare skin just above the collar of my smock.

'There,' I said, self-conscious now that he was still staring. 'Is that to your satisfaction?'

'It fits with my instruction,' said Marcus, finally looking away. 'There's apples in the bottom of that sack, if you are hungry.'

'Apples?' I said with excitement, forgetting all about the necklace. I hadn't tasted an apple in years. They were a real delicacy, rarely brought to our shores. The thought of having a whole one to myself had me rifling back in the sack.

Selecting what felt like the biggest, I held it up heartily. It was so red, so shiny. Without as much as polishing it on my smock, I took a massive bite.

Marcus looked on with interest, though his eyes darted away as soon as I looked up to meet them.

'Excuse my manners,' I said, wiping the juice from my chin with my sleeve. 'It's just that I've not eaten today.'

'It's not that,' he said, now staring at my mouth. 'It's just that I've noticed that the people from your island . . . why, they have such white teeth!'

I wiped the juice from my chin as Marcus's own teeth flashed yellow beneath his beard.

I turned away from his gaze to finish the apple. But now I faced the ocean instead. Black, undulating water. Powerful, deep; unforgiving.

'You're afraid of the sea?' said Marcus, after observing me for several seconds.

I shrugged, trying to calm my nerves, realizing that I

was nibbling my apple core as fiercely as a rat. Marcus clearly knew that my people avoided the ocean at all costs. That instead of fishing, we scaled the vertical cliffs and sea stacks, harvesting seabirds and their eggs rather than venture out on the dark water.

My father was one of the few islanders who had sailed over the ocean. But in the end, it came back to claim him.

'Or is it the creatures that lie beneath that you fear?' Marcus continued, his voice teasing. 'Like the selkies? Seals that can come to land and take human form.'

I looked back at him incredulously. Was he mocking me? 'I'm not a believer in those old tales,' I said sharply, pulling myself together. To prove my point I threw the skeletal apple core over the side of the boat where it hit the water with a defiant plop. 'And when I rule the islands with Artair, we shall only promote modern thinking.'

'That's the boy who helped you into the boat?' he said, thoughtful now. 'You think you will go back there for him?'

'Of course,' I said indignantly, my cheeks colouring up. 'He balanced on the Maiden's Rock for me!'

When Marcus didn't react, I explained.

'It's this ledge that hangs right over the sea. Suitors balance there – on one leg. To prove they will make a worthy husband . . . it's a *very* dangerous thing to do.'

'No doubt very useful,' said Marcus disdainfully, making further adjustments with the rudder. 'If one needs a husband who balances on rocks.'

'That's exactly what I will need!' I said, annoyed that he was mocking the island way of living. 'A man to climb the cliff-face to harvest birds and eggs – to provide for our children. We will start a family when I return!'

'If you say so,' said Marcus, his concentration now on the steering.

But I was raging and we didn't talk again for several hours.

'Where are we?' I said when I eventually grew bored of staring out across the grey waves, at the sun setting pink behind the clouds. Marcus pointed a long finger into the far distance. I could just about make out a group of islands, larger than St Kilda.

'The Outer Hebrides,' he explained. 'Though we'll be sailing around them to get to the mainland.'

'That's where my father was from,' I told him, sitting up for a better look. Really, it wasn't as far away as I had been expecting.

'Should make it to Oban sometime tomorrow,' said Marcus, handing me a woollen blanket. 'I would get some sleep if I were you.'

'Then what?' I said, my eyes still tracing the islands. 'I thought you would take me to the merchant's house?'

'The seas are too unpredictable at this time of year to sail around the coast of Scotland,' he explained. 'You'll be taking a wagon for the rest of the journey. I'll be staying with my boat.'

'Then who will be taking me?' I said, agitated. 'You are familiar with this person who will travel with me the rest of the way?'

'Why would I know him?' shrugged Marcus. 'Likely, it will just be some errand boy – paid handsomely to deliver you all in one piece. But it will be a long journey – so get some rest while you can.'

'Will you not need me to take another turn at the helm?' I said, fighting back tears. The sun was dipping down in the west and I was now afraid of what tomorrow might bring.

'I'll manage,' said Marcus. 'Go on now, get some proper shut-eye.'

We had been lucky with the weather – a strong wind in the right direction and hardly a drop of rain since leaving the bay. This fast little boat would have us to the mainland by tomorrow.

Despite my trepidation, the motion of the boat eventually had me nodding off. My last thoughts were of the sailor – and how he would stay alert all night to steer, now we were nearing rocky shores?

But that concern was all too soon to be answered.

I woke with a start, for a moment unaware of where I was. Above me, the dark sky was clear, leaving the crescent moon bright. The rocking motion confirmed that I hadn't dreamt the events of yesterday and that I was now many miles away from home, skirting along the rocky shores of western Scotland.

I looked round for Marcus, but to my shock I could see no one at the helm. It was then that I became aware of a lump of blankets a few feet away – and the rumblings of a man sleeping soundly. A man snoring his head off!

But how could this be? I sat up fully. How could a boat be left to steer itself through these waters?

Then I let out the loudest of screams. For the boat was not steering itself at all – there was a tiny creature manning the tiller.

'What is it . . . what's that?' cried Marcus, bolting out of his sleep. He sat up straight as I crammed myself into the narrow bow, as far away from the creature as possible.

'God help us,' I cried, pointing. 'There's a devil at the helm!'

At this the devil also emitted a loud noise, like the gurgle of a gannet. So this was what had made the strange noise in the bay last night!

I dug my nails into my palms, trying to catch my breath.

Noises that were not human. Innes had been right.

'It's OK, don't be afraid,' said Marcus kindly. At first, I thought he was trying to comfort me, but it soon became clear that he wasn't addressing me at all – he was talking to the thing! 'She's just an island girl – that's all,' he continued. 'Quite harmless, really. Let me introduce you two ladies – Nell, meet Iseabail. Iseabail, meet Nell.'

The devil made a familiar chattering noise and I looked up to take in the tiny darkened figure.

'What . . . is it?' I whispered. For it was by far the most terrifying thing that I had ever seen, despite it being scarcely two foot high – the size of a toddler. But it was no child, nor was it surely human.

'Make it go away,' I said, my voice no more than a hoarse whisper. 'Throw it over the side or something.'

At this Marcus became agitated. 'I'll throw *you* over-board before my little Nell, make no mistake,' he said angrily. 'How on earth do you think I've been sailing this thing for days on end through all kinds of weather? I'd be good and drowned by now if it wasn't for that "thing".'

Nell gave out an animalistic cheer whilst I lay help-lessly on the deck.

'Nell sleeps in the hold in the daytime,' Marcus said, pointing to the small cabin door at the back of the boat. I could make out the direction of his finger, but my eyes didn't dare follow to the fiendish silhouette cast across the helm by the moonlight. 'I've trained her to take over at night whilst I sleep,' Marcus explained casually, rummaging in his sackcloth. 'Here, take an apple, Nell,' he said to her. 'Have yourself a break . . . get to know our new stowaway.'

'No . . . please,' I insisted, but the thing did as it was asked, and its grotesque outline moved from the back of the boat to settle on the deck nearby.

I forced myself to look, my body convulsing in slow

horror at the arms carpeted in black hair and the moulded clay-like face. At first, I thought it was wearing a hood but now I saw that it was entirely covered in fur, its hairline reaching low over round black eyes which seemed devoid of white around the iris. Bizarrely, the creature wore a dainty green waistcoat – just like the one worn by Marcus, with matching shiny trousers.

The whole spectacle was diabolical.

'You do realize that she's a monkey,' said Marcus tiredly, letting out a long yawn.

'A monkey!' I repeated.

'I've trained her well, haven't I?' he said.

'A monkey!' I said again, for I was trying to think what such an animal might be.

'Yes, a m-o-n-k-e-y,' said Marcus, spelling out the letters like this would make more sense to someone so slow. 'It's a type of ape.'

'I know what a monkey is!' I said fiercely. 'I'm not stupid.'

And I wasn't lying, because now I thought of it, I'm sure Father had read me a story once about one. He said that they were intelligent creatures capable of all manner of tricks. But I needed to get a hold of myself! I wanted to prove that I wasn't just a meek island girl. I had to prepare myself for all manner of the unfamiliar in my year away from the island. I took a deep breath as Nell made a jabbering sound before biting into her apple with substantial-looking teeth.

'You were not supposed to wake up whilst she was working,' said Marcus with a little more sympathy.

'As long as there is nothing else shut up inside that cabin?'

'Nothing,' said Marcus, yawning widely, 'but a few crates of dried biscuit.'

At the mention of biscuits, Nell looked up from her apple.

'You can have some when your night shift is over,' Marcus instructed the monkey, whilst lying back down. 'She's wild about biscuits is our Nell. And I must get more sleep.'

'Really! You are to leave that thing in charge?'

'Well, you are far too inexperienced a sailor,' said Marcus, his voice muffled by his covers.

'And this animal . . . she knows the way?'

'You will find that this is not so unusual,' said Marcus drowsily. 'People train up monkeys for all kinds of tasks these days.'

Nell resumed her steering duties with an air of importance, looking out towards the shore to make adjustments. She didn't look my way again, but I sensed that I'd hurt her feelings.

'Stay up and stare if you like,' muttered Marcus from under his blankets. 'Just don't disturb me again.'

'No . . . I'll get some sleep now too,' I said steadily. 'We seem to be in good hands.'

I had no idea why I said this – whether I was sorry for

insulting the monkey or was afraid she might scratch me with her horrid furry hands while I slept.

'Goodnight, Nell,' I added cheerfully to further confirm my faith in her abilities. I pulled the covers over my head so I didn't have to look at Nell any more. 'See you in the morning!'

At some point, I fell back to sleep.

I woke with a jerk. I'd been dreaming that a furry creature was clawing at my face but when I sat up I only saw a cloudless blue sky and Marcus steering at the helm; there was no sight of Nell.

'She's back in the cabin . . . asleep,' said Marcus. Then he pointed towards the shore. 'We've made good time.'

'What?' I said, getting up quickly. The boat was a good bit nearer to land and I could make out a harbour.

'But . . . we can't be here already!'

Nausea bloomed in my stomach as I realized that leaving Marcus was imminent and the second leg of my journey, to goodness knows where, would soon begin.

'But you'll not just leave me here,' I said. 'You'll make

sure I'm in good hands before you sail away.'

'Why don't you see if anyone has arrived yet?' said Marcus, taking one hand away from the steering to root around for something. He held out a short metal tube.

I reached over and took it from him. It was lighter than it looked, like it was hollowed out inside. 'What is it?' I said, taking it from him. 'And how will this tell me if someone has arrived?' I thought that Marcus was playing a trick on me, something that would once again make me feel dumb and unworldly.

'It won't *tell* you,' said Marcus. 'But it will *show* you.' He took the rod back and held one end over his right eye. 'I think that I can see our man there, waiting on the beach,' he announced. 'And there's his wagon and horses . . . all ready to go.'

I looked over at the beach and squinted my eyes. There were a few dark shapes in the harbour, but they were tiny, far too far away to make out such details.

'You're making it up,' I said indignantly.

'Here, you try,' said Marcus, lowering the metal rod. 'Go on, take a look.'

I took the rod back and held it up to my left eye. It was indeed hollow, though it had a disc of glass covering the end that pressed into my eyeball.

'Other way round,' said Marcus bossily. 'Look through the other end and close your free eye.'

I did as he asked but expected nothing to happen.

The metal formed a cold ring over my eye as I pointed

the rod towards the harbour. At first, I saw nothing but a blurry circle of light but several seconds later the glass disc at the end of the tube began to change form.

I dropped the rod into my lap with shock, for the scene Marcus had just described swooped right up on me, like it was happening right there in the boat, just a few feet away. A man sat in a cart pulled by two black horses. I could even make out his coat, his long black boots.

'Careful, careful now there,' said Marcus, angry now. 'You'll crack the glass dropping it like that . . . those things are not easy to come by, you know.'

'But . . . what is it?' I said, staring at the stubby length of metal lying in my lap. 'Is it some kind of magic?'

I had always prided myself on not believing in things that did not have a rational explanation. But this journey was testing me.

'No, it's just an eyeglass,' sighed Marcus. 'It makes far-off things seem closer, that's all. It's all to do with how the daylight hits the glass.'

'Let me have another look,' I said, fascinated now.

'Fine,' said Marcus. 'But no dropping it this time.'

'Why, it's wonderful!' I exclaimed.

But the shore was looming near now and I didn't need an eyeglass to make out the grumpy-looking man abandoning his cart to walk to the water's edge.

I looked to Marcus for reassurance as he helped me over the side of the boat. But he paid me no mind, heaving my trunk into the shallows where it floated momentarily before being hauled out and up across the sand by the wagon driver.

Marcus climbed back into his boat and picked up his oars.

'It's been a pleasure, Iseabail McCleod,' he said. For the first time, it seemed to me, he met my eyes properly – though I was too far away to see his expression. Then he leveraged the oars to turn the faded eye painted on the bow of his boat to face back out to sea.

'Goodbye.' I waved after him pathetically. 'Goodbye, Marcus Amanza.'

It took me a while to get used to being inland, for despite despising the ocean, not having it in my sights made me giddy, like a part of my soul had been wrenched clean away. Still, with every turn of the wagon's wheels, my excitement grew about arriving at the merchant's grand house.

But the wagon driver wasn't for giving anything away about my destination. For the entire journey, which took over a week, he barely responded to my constant questions and observations as the metal rims of the wheels bumped along the muddy tracks.

I was in awe of the forests, entire hillsides coated with beautiful trees but all the driver could muster was that they were 'full of bears'.

Then came the villages. Then towns with fine timbered houses. At a market square, butchers' shops dangled rabbits whilst bakers flaunted wafts of hot bread. Next to the shoemaker there was a shop brandishing a mixing bowl above the lintel of its door.

'What is it that place trades?' I said, pointing. There were no windows at the front or any sign of what it might sell. 'What kind of shop is that?'

To this the driver gave me one of his rare replies. 'An apothecary – makes up medicines and potions,' he said, sniffing the air sourly as we passed. 'Most of it is nothing short of witchcraft. You'll be finding out all about *apothecary* where you're going!'

But on the subject, he would not be drawn further.

One early morning and several coaching inns later, the horses started to pull the wagon over higher ground. The bleak moorland felt unseasonably cold, the dew hardened to a thick crust of frost. Abruptly, the driver pulled on his reins and pointed into the distance, at a grey line across the horizon.

As I focused, it revealed itself to be the sea.

Could it really be that we had finally run out of land? That we had crossed from one side of this vast country to the other?

'This is as far as I go,' he announced, swinging his boots off the wagon and dropping down heavily on to the hard ground.

But I didn't understand. The only signs of habitation were wisps of smoke curling up from a hamlet in the valley below.

'You can't just leave me here,' I said, indignant.

But the driver busied himself with hauling my trunk out of the back of the wagon.

'I'll freeze to death!' I said, looking wildly about.

'Through there,' said the driver, tipping his head in the direction of a copse of frozen trees. 'You'll find the house soon enough.'

It was then that I made out a pair of thin gateposts skirting the moor. Like ghostly stalagmites they pierced the slate-grey sky, their bases blending in with the iced heather. A rough path wound through the posts, down into the trees.

'Why not take me a bit further?' I protested. 'Surely your wagon could pass through those posts . . . or even just go around them?'

But something spooked the lead horse and it began whinnying and rearing up on hind legs, the other one following suit. The man calmed them in a foreign tongue before turning back to me. 'They won't go no further,' he sighed, his voice for the first time showing warmth. 'Neither will I, come to that.'

I could now see a tower sticking up beyond the trees. 'Why? What's in there?'

'I've already said too much, I'm afraid,' said the driver, climbing back up on to the bench seat.

'But really . . . you have said nothing much at all! You have not told me a thing about this place to which I must go alone!'

'Not my place to say,' he said, tipping his hat. 'Goodbye, miss. And God bless.'

And with that he jiggled his reins and his horses galloped off gratefully in the direction of the village.

I watched the wagon wind its way around the ridge where the track forked down to the village, the driver not turning nor faltering in his decision to leave me here. Tiny flakes of snow began to fall, icy wispiness coating the posts in eerie silence. Winter must come early here.

I took a deep breath and willed myself towards the trees. If I didn't get going then my bare toes would soon freeze.

The sealskin trunk slipped easily over the icy ground to the stone posts. If they were gateposts, then where was the gate? Maybe they were simply markers to where the merchant's land ended and begun.

Each post was shaved flat on four sides and tapered to a pinnacle which drew the eye to the metal grey sky, like a pair of fat needles. With one finger, I scraped the frost from the one to my left, uncovering a swirling pattern in the grain. But as I removed more frost, forms took shape. Individual images began to emerge, so numerous and intricate that at first I had mistaken them for the natural pattern of the stone.

Serpents, birds, beetles, a man with the head of a dog, another with the head of an eagle. Assuming they ran the length and breadth of the pillar, there must have been thousands of these strange pictures buried beneath the covering of frost. I turned and cleaned a patch of the other post, finding identical decoration there.

As my eyes grazed on the strange symbols, I found my fingers had wandered to the necklace. Was it me, or did I sense a crackle as I rolled it between my thumb and forefinger, like there was static in the air, that feeling before a storm? Unlike the horses, I didn't feel afraid.

Instead, my mind became effervescent, excited at the thought of what other treasures might lie in wait inside the merchant's estate.

Picking up one end of my trunk, I began to pull it the rest of the way down the snowy track.

The merchant's house consumed me as soon as I emerged from the trees, a mansion of terracotta brick and shimmering glass, dozens of crenellated chimney pots twisting up into the grey, feathered sky.

I dropped my trunk beside a tree in wonder, drawn towards the flattened arch in which the massive front door was embedded. To the left loomed the round tower I'd seen from the wagon, set on a small hillock, a tall spiky tree growing up closely to one side. The tower had three small clover-leaf windows running roughly vertical up one side but despite its height, failed to hold my attention. Instead, my eyes were drawn back to the sweeping panes of the manor house, staring at me like the unblinking eyes of a wasp.

How on earth did such windows stay in place? Cascading panes of diamonds, glittering black. The sight made me feel suddenly dizzy.

So stunned was I by the architecture that I didn't notice that the door had been opened until someone shouted to me. A short and wiry man with dark skin was standing on the step, waving me in impatiently.

'Are you Alexander Plaustrell?' I asked as I walked briskly to the door.

But the man didn't seem to hear me. Instead, he bowed fleetingly in a way that suggested servitude rather than manners, all the while fluttering his fine-boned hands like a sparrow taking a dirt bath.

I decided that he must be a servant though he was dressed extravagantly in a cotton shirt and red bloomers which stopped just above his skinny knees. He stared down disapprovingly at my bare, dirty feet as he ushered me across the threshold.

'I'm Iseabail McCleod,' I explained as he led me into the magnificent hallway. The ceiling and walls were completely encased in shiny walnut panels and an elegant staircase swept down from the upper levels, its balustrade ending in a flawless curve. 'The merchant is expecting me.'

'*Santa Maria!*' he tutted, looking down at the pristine floor which was laid with an eye-crossing design of chequered tiles. '*Attento al mio pavimento!*'

'I'm sorry,' I said, feeling too weary now to be

ashamed of my naked feet. I realized that the servant hadn't understood a word that I said, nor had I deciphered anything that had passed from his impatient lips. What would I do if Plaustrell was not here and his daughter could not speak my language? Suddenly I felt faint and badly needed to sit down.

But then, without warning, a gangly dog the size of a pony flew down the stairs, closely followed by a wild-haired child.

'Whitefoot, Whitefoot!' the child cried out in Gaelic as she hitched up her yellow dress to navigate the stairs. She looked to be about eight years old, and despite her mass of hair was still smaller than the dog. I assumed her to be the merchant's daughter. 'Come back here!'

The dog paid her no mind and bounded towards an archway, its paws skittering to turn on the smooth tiles. But then it changed direction sharply and ran straight towards me, knocking me clear off my feet. I fell hard on to the polished tiles.

'You naughty thing!' cried the girl, attempting to pull the dog off me. But it was licking my face, great rivulets of slobber running down my neck. 'Get off that dirty peasant!'

Finally, the girl managed to extract the dog whilst the servant pulled me back on to my feet.

'My name is Iseabail McCleod,' I said, trying to neaten my smock. I was quite unharmed but now felt light-headed, compounded no doubt by the confusion of the girl's welcome. 'I've travelled many miles – at the behest of Alexander Plaustrell.'

The girl gaped at me in disbelief as the servant hauled the dog off to another room. Then she walked around me briskly, wrinkling up her nose as she took in my rough clothes and dirty feet. Thank goodness I'd had the sense to leave the seal-skin trunk outside. Finally she came to a halt right in front of me, her sweet, musky perfume invading my nostrils. 'Prove it!' she ordered.

I pulled the pearl from underneath my smock, hoping it would serve as evidence of my identity.

At this her eyes immediately softened. 'Thank the Lord that you arrived safely,' she said, mesmerized by the white pearl. She looked up at me with joy, a wide smile spreading across her lips. 'Welcome, dear Iseabail McCleod!'

Then she flung herself at me, her ringlets smothering her face as she pushed into my smock.

I swayed taking the weight of her, suddenly feeling hot as well as faint.

But I could not hold her for long. And whether it was the exhaustion of my long journey – or the mossy undertone of her cloying perfume – my legs buckled and I fell back to the floor, taking her with me.

When I awoke I was in a bed, a huge one surrounded by curtains. Shafts of daylight slotted through the gaps but whether it was the same day or next, I had no idea.

I sat up, causing my head to throb, finding a fine white cotton nightdress had replaced my rough smock.

Unsteadily, a hand came through one side of the curtain, laying itself gently on my arm. The hand was tanned, veiny and old and was shortly followed by a matching, wrinkly face.

An old woman had been sitting on a chair by the bed and now she stood to press both hands gently on my chest, indicating that I should lie back down. Her skin was so crinkled that it was hard to make out her features and I wondered if she might be one hundred years old.

I did as she indicated, my head as heavy as a rock. Now I remembered arriving in the merchant's house and I wondered if I had struck it on the tiles when I fell to the floor the second time; I prayed that the child had not been hurt too.

The old lady put a cool flannel on my forehead, all the while mumbling incoherently in the foreign language. I realized that I had not injured my head at all but was in the midst of a fever. The nightdress was stuck to my chest with sweat and my throat stung, raw and dry.

The ancient maid stood stiffly and pressed her hands to her own chest. 'Sylvia,' she said with a wary smile, her voice rolling and melodic. Then she left the room, returning moments later with the girl in tow.

The child was excited and looked to launch herself at me again, but Sylvia caught her deftly by the sleeve. The girl glanced up sharply at the nurse but was chastened enough to approach the bed with reserve.

'How are you, dear Iseabail?' she said, shooting Sylvia another angry look. The old lady curtsied and retreated with backwards steps from the chamber, her head bowed so that only the top of her grey cap was visible.

The girl pulled back the bed-curtains fully and sat down eagerly on the edge of the mattress. 'Sylvia said that you have taken a fever.'

'Yes,' I croaked, my throat aching badly, though I was now distracted by the magnificence of the bedchamber unfolding behind her.

'Papa said this might happen,' said the girl wistfully, touching my brow. She looked down at me with olive-brown eyes, her tawny cheeks framed by thick ringlets. 'That people from remote places easily catch diseases.'

'Diseases?' I whispered, alarmed, remembering how the merchant's letter spoke of the plague taking his wife.

'Oh, Sylvia says it is nothing to worry about,' the girl assured me. She spoke with authority and seemed very grown-up for a child. 'Just a sniffle, no doubt caught from one of those dreadful taverns. But don't worry, this house is a place of healing, you will be recovered in no time.'

I nodded, though personally I had found the roadside taverns to be the height of luxury – I had been fed thick, meaty stews, slept on straw-stuffed mattresses. But these extravagances were trifling compared to those found in the merchant's house.

Here I was now, lying on the softest bed and being

waited on hand and foot by a servant! But the opulence of the bedchamber made me worry that my trunk had been found. What if it had been hauled upstairs with all its simple, fetid contents rattling about inside?

I attempted to sit up to look but the girl tucked the sheets firmly back around my neck. 'Now you must keep warm,' she said, taking sole charge of my convalescence. She was wearing the perfume again but my blocked nose rendered it less pungent. 'The snows are here early – and the berries forecast a hard winter.'

'The berries?' I said, my throat aching with every word.

'Yes, the berries!' said the girl, like she was teaching me a fact. 'So many of them this autumn – a foreteller of a cold snap, that's for sure.'

I nodded again, thinking how this must explain the early snowfall.

'I can't wait to show you around when you are better,' the girl went on. 'The gardens, the tower . . . and the library, the chapel . . .' But then she stopped to snatch breath. 'But listen to me . . . jabbering on when I have not even yet introduced myself!'

At this she sprang up from the bed and took a dramatic curtsy.

'My name is Maria. Miss Maria Plaustrell. Aged seven and a half,' she breathed. 'Papa is still away travelling but I'll help you find your feet.'

'Maria,' I said, my own voice seeming faraway inside

my fever-ridden head. 'I don't think that I have heard that name before.'

'It's Italian,' she explained, collapsing back on to the bed. 'Just like me and Papa – like all the servants. Well, apart from that wretch of a stable boy – he comes from down in the village.'

I looked at her quizzically.

'Italy is a warm country in Europa,' she explained. 'Full of art and beautiful churches. We lived in Venice – a spectacular city that floats on water.'

I tried to imagine such a place, puzzled at why the merchant would move his entire household from this wonderful city to the frozen moor that lay beyond the lattice glass.

'Venice is a plague pit,' said Maria, reading my mind. 'Papa brought us here to escape disease – and because of the mineral spring, of course.'

She stood again, this time to fetch a glass tumbler from the dresser. She held it up to the light. It was filled with sparkling water.

'My health back in Venice was not the best but the waters here have worked wonders,' she said wistfully. 'Papa says they can cure *almost* anything.'

'You are sick?' I said with concern.

'I have bouts of weakness,' explained Maria. 'But doesn't everyone? That is why we all drink the water here, to keep healthy. In fact, we use it for everything – in cooking, laundry and, very importantly, bathing.'

'Bathing?' I croaked.

'Yes – a branch of the spring feeds directly into the bathhouse,' she said proudly. 'I myself take a hot bath every day . . . for my condition.'

Hot baths? Whoever heard of such a thing! The only wash I ever took was in the freezing burn that gushed down the gully into the bay.

'Sylvia will prepare our baths with restorative herbs and fragrances,' Maria went on. 'You will be required to take them too – we have strict cleansing routines here, to prevent the spread of diseases.' She approached the bed to press the tumbler to my lips. 'Drink now – it will make you feel better.'

I took a sip but the water just tasted ordinary. Much like our spring at home, though it maybe held a slight aftertaste. Noting I had had my fill, Maria drank down the rest of the water in one gulp.

I smiled in appreciation as Maria put down the empty glass and wiped my lips with a cloth. She was watching me carefully.

'Why, you have such white teeth,' she said finally, leaning towards me to see better. She seemed very pleased by this.

'It is common for my people,' I managed to reply, thinking of what Marcus Amanza had said.

'And your skin is so clear,' she continued, stroking my cheek like it was precious silk. 'No sign of disease.'

I noticed as her forehead caught the light that her skin

there was slightly pockmarked.

Then her eyes fell to the pearl that was still around my neck. 'Did Papa give you that?' she said, staring at it.

'The sailor that brought me from the island was instructed to do so,' I mumbled.

'It's lovely,' she said dreamily, her fingers reaching out to it. But she stopped short of touching the stone. 'Papa told me to look out for it – to make sure that the girl who arrived at the door was the one that had been chosen.'

'What country are we in here?' I said, changing the subject and pulling away, fearing she might take the pearl from me. 'Your father's letter said something about borderlands but I didn't quite understand.'

At this the girl stood and strode energetically towards the window. 'Well, that all rather depends on the day!' she smiled, her curls bouncing as she leant across the wide sill to point out through the leaded glass. 'To the south, we have England!' she announced dramatically. 'Ruled by the *terrible* Elizabeth, ready to chop off our heads for being true to the Old Faith.'

At this Maria turned to make a gesture across her throat, using a forefinger as if chopping it through with an axe.

'To the north, Scotland!' she said, pointing to the opposite, windowless wall of the bedchamber. 'Thankfully it has a Catholic queen. But the borders are really neither one nor t'other – its people obey only laws of their own. And up here on the moor we are mostly left to our own devices.'

The next few days passed in a blur of cold flannels and hot broth. My fever worsened but, just as the nurse had predicted, it wasn't of the dangerous kind. The girl attended me as well as the old lady, bringing me infusions concocted from plants from the garden, marvellous herbs that calmed my flaming throat, a boiled flower head that stilled the ringing in my ears.

Maria said she had learnt all these things from her papa and I asked if it was true what the wagon driver had said, that her father was one of these apothecaries.

'What exactly did that wretched man say?' said Maria, spooning a wobbly liquid into my mouth with a flat spoon, visibly rattled.

'Nothing much, believe me,' I said, wiping my lips with a cloth. 'He was pretty insufferable to tell you the truth – hardly spoke a word the whole way from Oban.'

'Good,' said Maria, seemingly pacified. 'Because those villagers tell hateful lies.'

'He wouldn't bring me up to the house though,' I said, watching her carefully.

Maria put the spoon down and smoothed her dress. 'Wouldn't he now?' she said shortly. 'Well, that's because *he's* not allowed to . . . we don't allow just anyone to visit, you know. We strive to keep their vile phlegm at a distance, their deadly diseases from our door.'

'But he seemed to be afraid of something . . .'

'The villagers don't like the posts on the moor, that's

all,' sniffed Maria, regaining composure by tucking a piece of hair neatly back into her cap. I had to remind myself that she was just seven and a half years old. So much younger than my sister Eilidh, yet the way Maria spoke, the way she held herself was so much more grown-up. 'But they are just decorated stones – brought back by Papa from abroad. Anything different seems like witchcraft to those stupid villagers!'

I wanted to ask about the horses – why had *they* been so afraid to enter the estate? It must have been something other than strange symbols etched into a pair of posts that made them rear up like that. But Maria was in full flow.

'Besides, the whole valley down there is riddled with Protestants,' she announced whilst holding up the set of beads dangling around her collar. 'These are called rosary beads and Catholics here wear them in prayer.'

'I'm afraid that we don't wear them on the island,' I replied. 'But we still pray to the Lord,' I added quickly.

'It must have been hard to leave your family all the way out there,' she said, lowering her beads. 'Your mother and your father?'

'Oh, I don't have a father,' I said coolly, taking the opportunity to tuck my own necklace tightly under my nightgown to avoid further scrutiny. Although it was just a piece of leather and a sea-pearl, I was becoming rather fond of it. 'And my mother and younger sister . . . well, we said our goodbyes.'

I thought that it was best not to mention Artair – or

my absolute intention to return home – because the little girl already seemed to have grown quite attached to me.

'But I am here now, Maria – and I will be a good companion to you, that is, as soon as I am well.'

'I know I can't replace your sister,' said Maria. 'But we will have great adventures. And we have a marvellous library at our disposal!'

Despite my lingering headache, the mention of a library caused my head to surge with adrenaline.

'I'm afraid I can read only a little,' I said, leaning back heavily on to my pillow. 'And mostly only in Gaelic.'

'All the important books are written in Latin,' explained Maria. 'But don't worry, Father Ronan will arrive soon to instruct us both.'

'I am to be educated?' I said, the thought swimming before my eyes.

'Certainly,' said Maria. 'And you will be moved into your proper room tomorrow . . . this one here belongs to Papa.'

'This is your father's bedchamber?' I said, shocked, sitting up sharply.

'Of course,' said Maria, taking the opportunity to plump up the pillows behind my back.

'I mean . . . I knew this wasn't *my* sleeping quarters,' I blurted out. 'But I never dreamt that they belonged to—'

'Don't worry,' said Maria. 'Get some rest now. In the morning, I will show you round properly. Now I must go for my bath – Sylvia will have heated the water by now.'

'I am sure to sleep well,' I said, slumping back heavily into the luxurious mattress and wondering when I would be required to take one of these strange hot baths.

But also, I couldn't help feeling disappointed that this wasn't to be my room after all. I had lain here since the day of my arrival and I was guilty of becoming accustomed to its opulence. I caught a glimpse of the grand marbled fireplace before Maria tugged the bed-curtains closed. Would they put me in the kitchen with the servants? I wondered.

'Goodnight, sweet Iseabail.'

I waited until the latch clicked shut, then sat up and pulled back the rich brocade.

So, this room belonged to Plaustrell: the mysterious merchant seeking a girl pure of heart; the man who sealed his scrolls with a lion of wax.

It was then that I noticed the delicate embroidery on the bed-curtains; it was made up entirely of woven lions! There must have been thousands of them, each one painstakingly stitched on to burgundy cloth with exquisite gold thread, each creature rearing up on tufted legs, tongues curling out from ferocious little mouths. And now the fireplace tiles became clear too: they featured the same image, each one stamped at the centre with an identical beast.

I lay down and stared at the underside of the canopy. I wondered when I would meet this man who had spirited a seventeen-year-old girl away from her homeland – just to accompany a coddled child. It was evident that he hadn't informed his daughter that I was only here temporarily. Why else would she ask about my family in a way that would suggest I might never see them again?

Still, I had to admit that, despite my illness, I was enjoying my time here: the supreme comfort – all the things of wonder, the prospect of exploring the merchant's estate. My intentions to make the most of every opportunity here were galvanized.

I closed my eyes, sleepy again, all the tiny images of lions still embedded in my vision. How they swam behind my closed lids, pranced around in my mind's eye.

Then I recalled an etching I had been shown of a lion once, which is why I had been able to identify the animal. It had been in a Bible belonging to one of the travelling priests that visited the island in summer to baptize the babies. The words that accompanied the picture came back to me clearly:

It will not lie down till it eat of the prey; and drink the blood of the slain.

The next morning, the girl was waiting by my bed as I woke.

'Are you ready to see your new room?' she said, pressing her hands together in one of her thrills. 'I'll help you to dress first if you like.'

I looked around, expecting to see my dreaded trunk, but instead there was an extravagant outfit laid out on a chair complete with undergarments.

'Do you like it?' Maria breathed, stroking the rich velvet as she helped me into it. 'Father brought it all the way from Spain.'

'Are you sure this is for me?' I said uncertainly, but obediently stepping into it. I had expected to be clothed in a manner similar to the old nurse with a plain gown and apron, but these were the robes of a noble lady.

'Of course,' said Maria, cheerfully fixing up the back fastenings. 'It's fairly chilly outside and I wanted you to be warm when we explore the garden . . . Is the dress not to your liking?'

'No . . . I . . . love it?' I began warily. 'It's just . . . a little big, that's all.'

'I'll get Sylvia to take it in for you,' said Maria, urging me to take a spin. 'You are a skinny little thing.'

'But . . . I surely cannot wear such a fine gown!'

'Why not?' said Maria haughtily. 'There is no one else to give it to. Papa brought it back from one of his voyages – it has not even been worn. It would give him such pleasure to know that you can find use for it.'

'Of course,' I said, bowing my head, realizing that I must have seemed most ungrateful. I had upset Maria and her cheeks had flared with red spots, the skin around her neck taking on a mottled look. 'Thank you for your generosity.'

Pacified, Maria's colour returned to normal. She stood behind me and fixed my hair, then steadily placed the matching coloured cap over my head.

'There,' she said, all bright again. 'You look perfect! Now we are ready to join the others for prayer. After which, I'll show you where you are to sleep tonight.'

Prayers were taken in a concealed chamber just off from the upper landing. I did not see its entrance until Maria clicked open a wall panel and the door sprang out from nowhere.

'This is our chapel, where we take Mass,' said Maria. 'Only those who live here know about it – and our visiting priest, of course. We're waiting for Father Ronan to arrive, so for now we just come here to pray.'

'What happened to the last priest?' I asked, but Maria didn't reply.

The chapel was crammed with the other members of the household, already gathered to pray. The servant who had first greeted me stood towards the front with two other men, also dressed in white shirts and scarlet pantaloons. Behind stood the old nurse, Sylvia, along with several barely younger women, and finally, at the back was a ginger-haired young man. This must have been the stable hand that Maria had mentioned as hailing from the village, though I found it odd that she had referred to him as a boy, despite him being closer to my age.

All the rest of the servants shared the same olive skin, thin bones and shiny grey or brown hair and all the men were clean-shaven. I tried hard not to stare at all the bare faces as Maria ushered me to the back of the room, pressing something hard into my hands before she took her place up towards the front.

I felt puzzled at why she should leave me at the back, but as the rest of the household knelt on blue cushions to pray, carrying out all sorts of murmured prayers and hand gestures, I realized that Maria wanted me to be able to watch and learn without feeling self-conscious. The thing she had pressed into my hand, when unravelled, revealed itself to be a string of beads identical to her own. One by one, the rest of the household revealed their own set which they twiddled dexterously in the ritual of prayer. I had seen such beads before when the priests visited our islands but had never owned a set before.

I held my beads and tried to follow, but mostly I just stared around the secret chapel, for what it lacked in size it made up for in reckless decor.

The panels of the walls were inlaid with vibrantly painted scenes, some of which I recognized from my fleeting teachings from the Bible: Jesus feeding thousands with just a few loaves and fishes, the Virgin and her Child, Moses on a cloudy mountain-top receiving God's tablets, and several others whose tales I couldn't fathom. The main characters were painted wearing vivid blue, their faces captivated with ecstasy or pain.

At the front there was a monumental altar encased beneath serrated pinnacles of wood growing down from the ceiling. At its centre was a heavily carved cabinet on which stood a solid gold cross. More strangely, a silver cast of an arm stood next to it, its finger pointing up to heaven.

How very opulent, I thought, the worship of these Catholics. Prayers back at home were held within an ancient arc of stone. There was no building that could claim to be a chapel.

I tried to concentrate on prayer, but when I looked up the stable boy had turned and was watching me. He studied my incompetent fumbling with the chain of beads with interest before winking and turning back to face the front.

Although I was mortified, his wink had been more of an encouragement than an inappropriate gesture. And I remembered Maria saying he was from the village. So he was an outsider here, just like me.

When we finally filed out, I loitered near the door, hopeful of making conversation with him. But Maria was already standing waiting. She took my arm firmly and let me back down the corridor.

After the prayer ceremony, Maria showed me my new quarters.

I had expected to be led off to a less grand part of the house, but instead she took me back past the merchant's bedroom and down a slightly narrower corridor that branched off from the landing.

'Close your eyes,' she instructed, holding my hand tight after stopping outside a door. Despite the fires burning everywhere in the house, her skin was cool and clammy. 'I do so hope that you like it.'

And with this, she pushed the door, led me inside and bade me open my eyes. I gasped, for the room in front of me was every bit as magnificent as her father's! Within it sat yet another carved four-poster bed, a black stone-flagged fireplace and beautifully carved furniture.

'We thought it best you used Papa's bed when you were sick,' she said, gauging my reaction as suitably impressed. 'To keep this one fresh for when you were well again.'

'But won't I be sleeping with the . . . other servants?' I said, wondering if this was a test or a game the little girl wanted to play. 'I mean, this bedroom is meant for . . . a lady.'

'And that is how Papa wants you to be treated,' said Maria, dancing across a spectacularly woven rug.

'But . . . I mean . . .' I began, daring to touch the exquisite bed quilt with the tip of one finger. 'This bed is all for me?'

'It's very comfortable,' said Maria, proceeding to jump on it. 'But Papa thought that we could sleep in here together, if you like, that is. There is lots of room. Look, there's even a bed for Whitefoot in the corner.'

Sure enough, there was a stuffed sack big enough to take the huge canine. After sharing a tiny bunk with

Eilidh, I could accept any roommate, even a dog the size of a horse.

'That would be wonderful,' I said, genuinely – for the room felt so big and detached from the rest of the house that it would feel lonely to take it all to myself.

'And of course, these are all yours,' said Maria, leaping from the bed and pulling me over to a recess covered by cloth. 'From now on, you can choose what you want to wear for the day, though I will want to guide you.'

And at this she pulled back a swathe of cloth concealing an annexe crammed full of fine clothing. Inside hung richly coloured dresses, skirts of pure silk, gowns of velvet, capes trimmed with animal fur.

'Isn't it marvellous that you can make use of Mama's clothes,' she went on, running her hand up and down the heavenly gowns whilst I gaped like a codfish. 'How I wish I was big enough to wear them.' She looked me up and down carefully. 'Though they will require some alteration.'

'They belonged to your mother?' I whispered, intimidated.

Maria nodded.

'No . . .' I began. 'Surely not . . . I cannot accept them.'

At this Maria stopped dead and turned to face me fully, a piece of purple silk still held tightly in her hand. 'You do not like them?' she said, slowly dropping the fabric so that the dress to which it was attached rustled back into the wardrobe. 'You would rather wear the rough clothes of a peasant?'

Once again, I was left feeling most ungrateful and yet yes, I would have preferred to be given the clothes of a maid, anything to clarify my true place here. Had the merchant really sanctioned my sharing of his daughter's bed and the daily parading of his dead wife's clothing? It seemed so unlikely. Maria was only seven and a half, I reminded myself. Was this anything more than a child's dressing-up game?

'I mean to say . . . that I am most grateful but . . . I could not possibly accept,' I said firmly.

I expected that I would be truly reprimanded but Maria burst out into hefty sobs. She ran back to the bed and flung herself face down upon it.

'Papa said that this might happen,' she said between wet sobs, kicking her legs up and down wildly. 'You don't like it here. You hate me and you hate this house! You don't want to be here at all, do you?'

Stunned at this outburst, I looked about the bedroom, at the rich furniture and tapestries plastered around the walls, at the leaded window, at the china vase over-flowing with orange orchids. It was so beautiful, more than I could ever have hoped for. The merchant had promised a life of luxury for the chosen girl, he was simply delivering on that promise. Maria was so distressed now, crying so hard that I feared she would stop breathing altogether.

'No, no, no,' I said, taking a deep breath and settling on a seat beside her. 'Why, my old house . . . well, it really can't compare. This house . . . this bedroom . . . why, it's the best I've ever seen.'

'Is it?' said Maria between sniffs. When she glanced up at me, I noticed the distinctive red spots had risen again on her cheeks and neck. 'Is it better than from where you are from? Will you not be too homesick here?'

'It is so much better than where I am from,' I said, thinking of the contents of my trunk and hoping that wherever it had been taken, no one had opened it. 'It's just that I'm not used to being in such a place. I'm only upset because . . . I . . . grew up surrounded by the ocean and I have not seen it for so long.'

I interjected this last bit to explain my discomfort at living in such a luxurious house, though there was of course some truth in it.

At this Maria stopped sobbing and jumped down from the bed, her colour slowly returning to normal.

'Look, look!' she said, urging for me to follow again. 'Papa has already thought of everything!'

She stopped by the window this time, one hand pointing out fiercely through the glass.

I followed her tentatively wondering what treasure she might reveal this time.

'Here is your ocean,' she said proudly, stepping aside so that I could look. 'Every time you are homesick, you can look out right here.'

Through the window I could make out in the distance the thing the wagon driver had shown me. A pale grey line on the horizon almost indistinguishable from the snow-covered moor.

'That is the North Sea,' Maria said airily. 'I myself have sailed over it before.'

'I'm afraid that it's too far away to look like my sea,' I said, leaning into the sill as Maria moved the vase of orchids to one side. What little I could see of the flat grey ocean was chopped into fuzzy diamond shapes by the lattice glass; it was a world away from the white crashing waves of the Atlantic.

'I told you,' said Maria, now across the room again and fumbling in a drawer. 'Papa has thought of *everything*.'

Seconds later she was back, holding out a familiar-looking metal tube. Just like Marcus Amanza's but the tube was a little longer.

Confidently, I took it from her and held it up to one eye.

'You know what it is for?' she said, taken aback, whilst I opened the latch in the window for a better view, letting in an icy blast.

'Of course,' I said, taking care to put the right end to my eye this time. 'I have seen an eyeglass before, you know.'

And although still underwhelmed by the magnified grey ocean, stilted like flat iron on the horizon, its presence renewed my confidence, cemented my resolve that I would stay strong, make the most of my experience here before returning home to my own shores.

That's what I thought, at least, as I stared through the eyeglass across the borderlands at the pitiable North Sea. If only I could have seen what really waited on my own horizon, if only I could have seen the true horror that lay ahead.

The next morning, Maria showed me the merchant's estate. More unseasonable snow had fallen overnight: as we stepped on to the frozen ground, it felt more like February than late autumn.

First Maria showed me all kinds of animals kept at the back of the house and beautifully coloured wandering birds called peacocks which stood out drastically against the snow. Maria said that the house was almost self-sufficient with only flour for bread having to be brought up from the village and goods sent back from the merchant's travels to supplement the larders.

The orchard was breath-taking, despite being

suppressed by the chill of the early winter, and Maria's descriptions of how it would look come summer conjured up trees heavy with sunburst fruits, thrumming with honey bees and blossoms, from the lines of skeletal branches.

The kitchen garden was vast and walled, with never-ending furrows for cabbages and beets lying dormant beneath a crust of frost. Clustered around the perimeter sat cribs in suntraps, poised for growing precious herbs come the spring.

I pointed to a trough jutting out from an archway of stones.

'What's that?' I asked, expecting it to be ready to house yet another kind of plant or vegetable.

'Oh, that's one of the branches of the mineral spring,' explained Maria as we walked over to the trough. 'The reason why Papa bought this entire estate.'

The water emerged from a pipe hammered into the bedrock, a trickle fusing into the frozen pool in the trough, which was emblazoned – like so much else on the property – with Plaustrell's lion motif.

I pulled my hand from my rabbit-fur glove and touched a finger to the icy trickle.

'It's the same stuff as you've been drinking since you arrived here,' said Maria.

'So it is,' I said, warming my finger in my mouth, recognizing the faintly metallic notes. 'I mean, it's good – but wouldn't you say that it holds a certain aftertaste?'

Maria looked pleased with my observation. 'That's because it has drained through special rocks,' she said taking off her own glove and cupping her hand below the trickle. Then she drew her hand up towards her lips and tipped the liquid into her mouth. 'Papa says that's what gives it healing properties. The main spring is channelled directly into the bathhouse.'

I had already experienced the bathhouse, having been encouraged to take my first dunking there yesterday evening. It was a wondrous room which sat behind the kitchens so that the warmth from the ovens could be used to heat the water. Maria explained how this was possible, but I was more enraptured by the steamy room itself, its ceiling billowing with fine muslin sheets filled with petals and sweet green herbs. The tub itself was wooden and secured to one wall into which fed two pipes of water – one hot and one cold.

But I hadn't enjoyed the experience of the bath so much. I had been attended by Sylvia who had insisted on the water being almost scalding and proceeded to scrub my back hard with lye soap. She seemed astounded at the dirt that had come off me.

'But how did he manage to purchase the land?' I asked Maria as she replaced her glove, thinking of the amount of this precious resource the household must get through. 'Surely the villagers must know of the spring's existence?'

'The locals know of the water's benefits only too well –

but something else kept them from living up here on the moor. Come look!'

Maria pulled me out of the walled enclosure and down through a sunken garden. This brought us out at the hillock atop which the ancient tower was perched. Here she showed me the distinctive tree I'd noticed the day I'd first approached the house.

It was a strange tree, even to my untrained eye, with spindly branches weighed down by the snow. The lower branches almost brushed the ground, but their tips still curled stubbornly skywards, like shepherd's crooks.

'The tower and the tree were already here when Papa bought the land,' reported Maria. 'But because the tree is so unusual, the locals believe it cursed the whole place.'

I looked up at the tree which had grown almost as high as the tower. 'Why not just cut it down then?'

'They say that it cannot be felled,' she replied, her voice becoming mysterious, 'because the Devil lives in the trunk – and he will escape.'

'The Devil?' I laughed uneasily. 'And the villagers believe this?' But there was something off about the tree. Not only were the branches sinister, but the bark on the trunk seemed unnatural, running in perfectly smooth patches before erupting in sharp, concentric waves. It might persuade the most even-minded of people that there was something trapped in there, trying to claw its way out.

'The locals are terrified of it,' laughed Maria, throwing back her head. 'They say that even its shadow can bring on nightmares. But Papa says he's seen these trees growing in hot countries. They are nothing to be afraid of.'

'But how would such a thing get here?' I continued, not completely convinced. Maybe this was the reason that the wagon driver had refused to enter the estate.

'I don't know. But Papa has travelled the world – he knows *everything*,' continued Maria with conviction. Then her face took on an impish look. 'He claims that the leaves are so sharp they can pierce the hide of a cow.'

'I'll take your word for it,' I said, turning to walk away, but Maria deftly caught one of my gloves, wrenching it from my hand. 'I dare you to touch it, Iseabail!'

'Thank you, but no,' I said, going to retrieve my glove, but Maria snatched it out of reach again.

'Don't be a spoilsport,' she said, angry now, the colour rising on her cheeks. 'Now touch it – I order you!'

Reluctantly, I approached the tree. I supposed that I had been brought here to be the girl's companion and this, along with her dressing me up, was just another one of her little games. Surely the leaves weren't as sharp as her father claimed.

Carefully, I placed my thumb against the spine of a leaf, surprised to find it was as hard as bone, its ridge as sharp as the edge of a broken seashell.

'Press harder,' she said, joining me at the tree and pushing her own gloved hand down over my thumb. 'Do it properly!'

'Stop!' I said, feeling a sharp painful scratch. Maria stepped away – but it was too late. As I snatched my hand away from the tree, two fat beads of blood spouted from the bulb of my thumb.

Maria watched them drop to the ground, obviously fascinated, a shard of glorious redness bursting across the snow.

I turned away, sucking at the injury furiously, then gathered up my glove that she had let drop to the wet ground.

'I didn't mean for you to bleed,' she cried out peevishly. 'Now don't you dare sulk!'

'Let's just say that the leaves live up to their reputation, shall we?' I said as coolly as I could, turning and starting to walk away. I wouldn't let it show that she had hurt me. She had made me bleed on purpose and I would not give her the satisfaction of my anger.

Instead, I ran up the seven snow-encased treads of the tower steps. Breathing deeply, I swallowed my fury.

'That's Papa's workshop,' Maria called up at me. She had trailed me to the base of the steps, but I did not turn to listen to her. 'No one is allowed in there – and he keeps it locked when he is away.'

I stood with my arms folded, staring at the entrance to the tower. The wooden door was patched with frost, its black metal handle furry with icy crystals. It looked like it hadn't been opened for quite some time.

'I snuck inside once when Papa was home,' continued

Maria boastfully, as I craned up at the vertical line of three windows, their clover-leaf panes reflecting black and unlit. Up close the tower showed its age, lichen and moss carpeting the cracks of the curved stones. 'But he caught me.'

I wanted to ignore her, poking a lichen frozen to lace, but badly wanted to know what she had seen in there. However, the girl, desperate to regain my favour, answered my unspoken question.

'He wasn't too pleased,' she went on feverishly. 'I hardly had time to look at a thing before he shooed me out.'

'But what did you see?' I asked, curiosity superseding my sulk.

'Treasures from all over the world,' said Maria. 'Strange creatures, animal skins . . . rolls of ancient parchment.'

'What else?' I demanded, still without turning.

'Disgusting things floating in jars,' she added, now revelling in my interest. 'And books piled high. My eyes hardly had time to take it all in. But I'll tell you all about it back inside the house. Come now, it is beginning to snow again!'

'There's more books in the tower?' I said, as fat flakes began to fall again. 'Why not keep them in the house, with the rest of his library?'

'He says that they are very old and delicate,' said Maria, wincing as a tiny maelstrom stung her face. 'And that there is no point in letting anyone else look at them as they are written in alphabets that few understand.'

'There are other kinds of alphabets?' I asked, fascinated now, planting my boots firmly in the compacted snow the wind had pushed up against the door.

'Greek, Cyrillic, Chinese and others long forgotten since ancient times,' announced Maria, raising her voice against the gathering squall. 'It takes Papa an age to read them, to work out of what they speak. Now do come along – I've lost all feeling in my toes!'

'I wish I could see them,' I said, touching the frosted door with my glove. I didn't care a jot about her toes – she was always moaning and making a drama about being cold. 'Even if I couldn't read a thing that they said.'

'I've told you already – Papa allows no one in there,' said Maria, stamping her boots on the ground in a bid to warm her feet. 'Besides, isn't there more than enough to keep us going in the library? Which is where I'm going before I freeze to death!'

At this, she stomped off over the frosty grass.

But I could not tear my gaze from the door. There was something magnetic about that tower. Something drawing me to it. A locked room that only one person was permitted to enter, full of ancient wonders collected from all over the world. And that beastly tree growing up beside it, reaching out its devilish branches in a bid to keep prying eyes away.

Reaching out on instinct, I scraped a patch of frost

away from the top half of the door with my glove. I was surprised to find the timber beneath to be smooth, un-splintered, not in keeping with the aged stone of the tower. Further scraping uncovered part of a carving.

My fingers soon traced out the rest of the outline, uncovering a familiar-looking lion rearing up in profile on tufted back legs, an oversized tongue curling from its mouth.

The Lion Rampant.

I had already learnt from Maria the name of the figure that appeared all over the house. She claimed that it was a common symbol of heraldry, but the merchant seemed quite obsessed by it: from the wax seal he stamped on to his letters, to the delicate embroidery on his bedclothes. I wondered why it held such sway with him.

Then I noticed that there were letters engraved into the bottom of this particular carving which I had at first mistaken for the render of the animal's foot: A M A P. I traced the curling letters curiously with my finger, wondering what they could stand for.

But the wind had become bitter now and I was worried that Maria's temper would worsen if I didn't follow her back to the house soon. Glancing up at the lion one last time, I ran down the steps and followed Maria's dainty footprints dutifully back through the garden.

Father Ronan arrived on horseback a few weeks later from Melrose Abbey and it was I who witnessed his approach through the lattice glass of the upper landing. I was basking in the coolness of the velvet window seat, trying to fathom the Latin in a medical journal when I caught movement on the moor out of the corner of my eye. Maria, who was off taking one of her lengthy baths, would be peeved that she had missed his arrival.

The priest had been expected the day before and we had taken books up to the landing to occupy us whilst taking turns to watch over the moor. Now, in her absence, I observed the stoutness of both the rider in his flowing, hooded robes and his short-legged mountain pony. At the posts, the pony wavered, tossing its rough head this way and that, refusing to pass through. With obvious annoyance, the priest dismounted and urged the pony to circumnavigate the posts, rejoining the snowy track to bring them down into the trees.

Father Ronan proved to be a barrel of an Irishman with an affection for whisky. His slurred homilies would inadvertently recount (in unnecessary detail) some poor Catholic's execution. But I quickly developed an affection for the man, who was kind and clever, and had a refreshing lack of regard for the household's schedules. And although I would come to seek him out for conversation when the girl was taking her baths, his presence here still troubled me.

'Are you not worried that the Protestants will follow a priest here?' I whispered to Maria one afternoon whilst we were supposed to be taking Latin in the library. Father Ronan, having set us each a writing exercise, was now slumped over the bolster of the settee, sleeping fitfully. He had turned up to the lesson carrying heavy fumes on his breath.

'We are quite safe here in the borders,' said Maria, finishing a line of cursive with a flourish. 'Father Ronan says that Scotland has not yet fallen to the tyrants.'

'But what about England? Surely the borderlands sit within its reach?'

'Don't worry,' said Maria firmly. 'Papa has ensured

that the estate here is well protected.'

'Protected?' I queried, my own quill pausing in the air. Although I was enjoying what little Latin the priest managed to impart each lesson I was worried this came at a price. 'By what means?'

'I've already explained to you about the tree,' said Maria tersely, wiping her quill tip against the edge of the inkpot. 'And then there are the posts on the moor – even strangers to the area are afraid to enter through them. They offer us all the protection that we need.'

At the mention of the posts, Father Ronan stirred in his sleep, his fat fingers twitching, like he was flicking away serpents.

As I turned to observe the priest, Whitefoot, who was as usual lounging by the fire, took this as an invitation to slink over and lick my hand.

'It is their markings that induce fear,' continued Maria, eyeing Whitefoot then my hand suspiciously, as I discreetly pushed away his whiskery head. 'Even though no one understands their dead alphabet.'

'Those symbols – are an alphabet?' I said, now desperate for the dog to leave me alone. Maria couldn't stand it when the dog showed me such affection when he had nothing but barks and growls for her.

'Yes, it's ancient Egyptian,' announced Maria, her eyes back on her parchment. 'Papa says that the stones are called obelisks and that they once guarded the tomb of a desert king from robbers.'

Now I remembered that the pictures on the posts were carved in lines of sorts, as though they were indeed meant to be read like text. 'And what is it that they speak of?'

'Old magic,' replied Maria, without looking up from her study.

'Magic?' I repeated incredulously.

Father Ronan stirred again but was still not roused from his slumber.

'Shh!' she scolded, staring at me now. 'By old magic, I mean simply superstition. Surely that is the greatest deterrent of all.'

I thought of the rings of standing stones back on the island, some of which were scored with strange whirling marks. Some of the elders said that they had been put there by the faeries and that it was bad luck to use the stones for new buildings. It was this kind of thinking that Artair and I planned to curtail, yet those beliefs still held sway over many of the islanders.

'Don't you agree?' Maria went on, 'that the best form of protection is simple fear?'

'I suppose so.'

'Now how about a walk in the gardens?' she said, making to pack up her box of inks. 'I could do with taking some air before my bath. And I take it that you will be having one today?'

I nodded reluctantly, as we left Father Ronan sleeping and passed through the entrance hall to don our furs. Maria had figured out my dislike for baths and knew I would make excuses to get out of them.

But I wasn't worried about bathing; instead the words of the wagon driver had invaded my thoughts.

They won't go no further, neither will I.

'What about animals then?' I pursued as we worked our way through the back of the house to the kitchens. 'Why don't horses like going through the posts?'

'Animals pick up on the fear of their masters, nothing more than that,' said Maria airily. 'You'll learn all about that when you take your first riding lesson.'

I didn't mention Father Ronan's pony refusing to go through the posts. If it had picked up on fear for its rider, then was it the priest instead who was fearful? It certainly hadn't seemed that way.

We left through the doors of the kitchen, but just as we made to descend into the sunken garden, there came the snort of an animal. The red-headed stable boy rounded the edge of the tower, riding a sleek grey gelding.

'Velvet!' exclaimed Maria, running towards the horse which she had already told me was her favourite. 'Hey, you boy! Bring my horse to me!'

Looking stunned to come upon us, the boy cautiously brought the horse closer. His eyes locked with mine and we exchanged wary smiles. I had learnt that his name was William.

'When the snow melts I'll be able to exercise you myself!' said Maria, advancing on the animal, scorn in her voice for Velvet's current rider. 'Here, Velvet!'

But despite William's attempt to calm the horse by stroking his mane, the creature was spooked. He had reared up on hind legs before Maria was upon him. The girl fell backwards in shock and I caught her before she fell into the snow.

'Let go of me,' she said, squirming in my arms as the boy calmed Velvet with a series of tongue clicks. But the horse continued to whinny and back away from Maria with sharp steps. 'Am I not allowed to pat my own horse?'

'Velvet did not expect you, that's all,' I assured her as the animal stilled. 'You sprang right out of nowhere.'

I gestured for the horse to be taken away though I was sad that my encounter with William had been so brief.

'You just wait till my papa gets home!' Maria screamed at William as he rode the horse away back towards the stables. 'I'll tell him that you've turned my own horse against me!'

I managed to coax Maria down the steps and into the relative shelter of the arbour where she sat down at the bench furiously. But the colour in her cheeks was already changing, plum-coloured spots pulsing beneath her delicately thin skin.

'That wretched boy,' she mumbled through angry tears. 'I wish Papa had never taken him in.'

I approached the bench with reserve, disappointed once again that I had not been able to speak with William. Since our first encounter in the chapel, I had been desperate for a chance to meet the boy alone. Surely he would be the only person in this entire household who could understand how it felt for me to be here. Another young person, living away from their family.

It was as if Maria had read my thoughts. 'Iseabail, you must not engage with that boy,' she warned, as I took a seat beside her. The girl had regained some composure, straightening her back as she drew her furs closer, the red welts on her skin fading. 'Even when the snows thaw and he prepares our horses for riding on the moor. He's not one of us and he can't be trusted.'

'Because he is from the village? Because he is English?' I said, trying to understand her hate for him.

'Just because you have never heard him speak either Gaelic or Italian,' said Maria, her eyebrow arching incredulously, 'you assume that he must only speak English?'

'Yes,' I said, because I had already given great thought to the matter.

'For your information, he cannot speak English,' said Maria, with a look of satisfaction. 'Or any other language come to that!' She took great joy in watching me work it out.

'You mean . . . ?'

'That's right, the boy is a mute,' she continued, a cruel smile playing on her lips.

'I suppose that makes sense,' I said soberly, picturing William diligently thumbing his rosary during Mass. He always mouthed away at the psalms but it was true; I had never once witnessed him speaking out aloud and he commanded the horses using only tongue clicks. 'And you say that your father took him in?'

'Papa found him wandering on the moor when he was out riding one day,' said Maria, now basking in her story. 'He was half-starved and full of fleas. The villagers had banished him, you see. Because he survived the pestilence.'

'William survived the plague!' I said, astonished, sitting down beside her. The plague had never made it to our island, but we had heard of it – how it wiped out whole villages, decimating towns and cities. How hardly any poor soul that succumbed to it was spared.

Maria's nostrils flared with indignation at my use of his name. 'Yes, the villagers claim that the wretch survived the plague,' she spat. 'And that the Devil took his tongue as payment!' She glowered at me. 'You know his name . . . ?'

I knew that I had to tread carefully now. She was so close to taking another fit.

'I only know his name because one of the maids called him into the kitchens for food,' I explained, gently placing my hand on the sleeve of her coat.

'Well, of course he could not have told you himself,' she said, her voice hinting of glee.

I swallowed hard, stunned by her cruelty.

'But surely, Maria,' I began, forcing the words from

my lips. 'A clever, educated girl like yourself would not believe that the Devil took his tongue?'

'That is true,' she said, drinking in the compliment. 'Anyone that survives the plague is bound to be somewhat diminished. But what I do believe is that he's taken advantage of my papa's good nature!'

'But he's so good with the horses – surely that must be why he is allowed to stay?' I ventured.

'Or more likely the villagers have tricked us into taking him – so that they can spy on Papa's work!'

'You mean his work as an apothecary?' I said stupidly, without thinking.

'What do you mean?' said Maria, her forehead bulging with a fresh wave of anger. 'His work as an *apothecary*?'

'It's just that the wagon driver that brought me here—'

'*You* said that despicable man had hardly uttered a word for the entire journey!' cried Maria, standing furiously. 'Yet you seem to have discussed my father at quite some length!'

'Well, what I really think is just how merciful it was of your papa to take pity,' I said in a desperate attempt to placate her. 'When the boy's own family cast him out so cruelly.'

When I first arrived at the house, Maria was not so quick to anger, I was sure of it. These days almost anything could set off her tempers. She was now looking up at the frozen vines twisted into the metal arc of the arbour, her gloved hands clenched in fury. When her eyes met mine again, I feared that she might strike me.

But instead she took in a gulp of air and breathed it out slowly, like she was willing every fibre of her being to stay in control.

'I suppose that you are right, dear Iseabail,' she said evenly. Then she bent over to take my gloved hands into her own. 'You will find that Papa is really a most generous man.'

I was becoming adept at employing flattery to dispel her rages. Kind words about her father, this mysterious merchant I was yet to meet, usually did the trick.

'Well, I hope that I meet with his expectations,' I said. 'Pray that he finds me to his liking.'

'Oh, he is sure to be pleased with you,' said Maria, now completely composed and smiling in her strangely adult way. 'I am quite sure of it.'

'Maybe we should be getting back inside, Maria,' I said, standing up from the bench. Devoid of temper, her face looked pale and bloodless. 'Your lips are turning blue.'

'In a moment,' she said. 'It's just that I'd like to take this chance to tell you about Papa's work – dispel whatever myths you have heard.'

'It doesn't matter . . . really . . .' I began, trying to steer her out of the arbour.

But Maria was determined. 'It's a potion that Papa seeks to make, that's all,' she said, her gaze falling softly across the sunken garden. 'A potion that can cure the plague.'

My mind conjured up the strange apothecary shop the wagon trundled past on our journey here. The driver had said it was nothing short of witchcraft.

'Most victims die within days,' Maria continued morosely, like she was in a trance. 'Their blood poisoned to black.'

'Maria, please—' I began, but she stood her ground.

'The physicians' remedies are no more than cures for the common cold,' she said, her tone now bitter. 'Rubbing pustules with onions, burning herbs to purify the air – you might as well just bury the afflicted alive.'

I shivered at the thought of the plague, remembering that Maria's mother had herself died of the disease. I envisaged an older version of Maria – a beautiful Italian lady – dying in a grand, canopied bed. Her long dark locks strung with sweat across the finest silk pillows, a pretty face bursting with sores. The plague knew no bounds. The rich died as grotesquely as the poor.

'Their blood,' I said finally. 'It really turns black?'

'Dark as treacle,' said Maria brutally. 'Like the Reaper has already taken their souls and is just parading the living, rotting corpse.'

'Then how can there be a cure for such a terrible thing?' I said, shaking my head in disbelief. The people on my islands died easily when they became ill. And they believed that only God could spare you from death.

'Well, his potion almost worked,' said Maria solemnly. 'He was so close to saving Mama.'

'He used his medicine on your mother?'

'That he did – but all it did was prolong her suffering. She languished for weeks instead of days. But in the end, death refused to be cheated.'

An icy blast suddenly penetrated the arbour and I leant down to fasten Maria's furs closer about her neck, worried that she looked so cold.

'And you can remember all of this?' I said, thinking how I maybe should be more understanding of her outbursts. 'You must have been so young. Poor Maria.'

At this Maria suddenly embraced me, her small body holding on to me tightly. It felt like a long time since I had been held by anyone, and I wished suddenly and painfully that Artair's strong, warm embrace surrounded me, not the slender arms of this sick little girl.

'But at least there is hope for your papa's potion,' I said encouragingly, though her perfume had caught the back of my throat. 'If the medicine worked better than anything tried before, then maybe he just needs to change the ingredients a little. Maybe one day, he really will find a cure for the plague.'

'Clever Iseabail, you are so right,' whispered Maria, stroking my hair. 'That's where he is right now – in pursuit of his missing ingredient. If only it wasn't so rare.'

A few days later we were in the library waiting for our lesson to begin, but as yet there was no sign of Father Ronan.

The weather had not improved and mostly we were still confined to the house. I had quizzed Maria several times about her papa's whereabouts – and what rare ingredient he sought – but she feigned that she knew nothing further about the matter.

Maria, bored of waiting for the priest, had taken out her box of coloured inks and a fresh sheet of parchment. She was penning a book on herbs that heal and had completed the first three pages competently, complete with accurate drawings. She really was astounding for such a young girl.

'I don't think that we can count on seeing Father Ronan at all today,' I yawned, the roaring fire making me drowsy. 'Sylvia says that he was seen staggering around in the woods.'

'So you understand the servants now?' said Maria, stopping what she was doing to raise an eyebrow.

'I recognize a few phrases,' I confessed, knowing how she hated the thought of me conversing with anyone but herself. 'But mostly we communicate by pointing things out and miming.'

'Well, be wary of their tittle-tattle,' she said, satisfied, rifling through her quill box.

'How did your papa come to know Father Ronan in the first place?' I asked, standing to walk over to the lattice windows to escape the heat. I lay my cheek against the cold glass, drinking in the draughts, suddenly yearning for the dank air of the blackhouse.

'He's just a replacement for the last priest, though I'm sure the monastery just send us the idiots that are of no use to them.'

I turned to face her and she read my expression.

'I'm afraid priests don't last long here,' she sighed, selecting a black quill. 'It's too lonely up here on the moor.'

But I knew that clergymen were used to solitude. My father once told me that it was part of their training. It must be something else about this house that was driving them away.

Just then, a horn sounded on the moor.

'A messenger!' cried Maria, sitting up excitedly. 'Can you hear? Out at the posts.'

But the ground-floor windows in the library afforded only a view of the trees and so we both scrambled into the hallway.

'The boy will fetch the message for us,' Maria declared as she opened the front door wide, letting in fresh, cold air. Then she hopped about on one foot to the other. 'Oh, I do hope that it is news from Papa!'

Moments later, William passed by on a pony from the back of the house, galloping up into the trees to meet the messenger at the posts whilst we girls waited in the hall. Sylvia had joined us as well as Eugene, the flappy handed servant who had greeted me on arrival.

Soon after, William was back holding up a rolled parchment which Maria demanded was handed to her immediately. Then she slammed the door in William's face before we could even trade smiles, dismissed the other servants and ushered me back into the library.

'They're so nosy!' she declared as she shut us back into the heat of the room. 'Sit over there, Iseabail, and I will read it to you.'

As expected, the message was from the merchant and even though Maria would not let me too near to the scroll itself, I recognized that it was written in Latin. The sight of the familiar, wispy calligraphy brought a sharp lump to my throat.

'He promises to be home for Christmas!' she cried joyously. 'And Papa is a man of his word!'

'May I see?' I said, but the girl twisted away from me.

'And he'll bring a wild boar for the table,' she went on.

I decided to wait until she had read it, then ask again to see it myself. I wouldn't be able to read all of it as my Latin was still poor but I could at least see if he had mentioned my name.

But to my dismay, after Maria had finished with the letter (the silent reading of which she interluded with whoops of joy), she stood and threw the whole thing on to the fire.

'Did I ever tell you that crow-feathers are best for drawing fine lines?' she commented, sitting back up at her desk and picking back up the black quill as if nothing had happened.

'What else did the letter say?' I asked steadily.

'Nothing much,' said Maria, now scratching away diligently on the translucent calfskin. 'Only that he would be bringing me a special present.'

'Did he say what it might be?'

'No,' she said airily, dipping her quill again.

'Then why did you burn it,' I said slowly, thinking about whether or not the girl even knew of the promises her father had made to me. 'Why did you need to burn the letter?'

'Because it's private,' said Maria. Then added, 'And I don't want the servants to read it.'

I sat on the armchair furthest from the fireplace and picked up a pamphlet of Latin poetry. 'Which servants can read Latin?' I said evenly, sure that the only person she was hiding anything from was me.

Maria scratched her forehead with the feather end of the quill, thinking. 'I meant . . . Father Ronan,' she said dismissively. 'He's always poking his nose into things.'

'What about the rare ingredient?' I said, desperate to know anything at all about the rest of his message. 'Did your papa say he had been successful in tracking it down?'

'Papa's message was addressed to me, Iseabail,' she said, visibly rattled that I had once again brought up the subject of her father's potion. She re-secured one corner of her scroll with a weight to stop it from curling. 'What it contained is none of your business.'

I stared into the fire, my face boiling with heat and frustration. I was desperate to know if the merchant had sent the supplies he'd promised.

For although I had learnt many things here in his grand and wondrous house, not much of it seemed relevant to the life to which I would eventually return. Supplies to see my island safely through the winter would make coming here all worth it.

'I am so very glad to hear that your father is a man of his word,' I said gruffly, wondering if Maria was aware of *any* of promises that he had made to me. One thing was for sure, I would raise them the moment I had any privacy with him. 'Really, I can't *wait* for Christmas.'

Just then, Whitefoot let out a loud yawn from his cushion in the corner.

'That dog is such a lazy beast,' I said, standing to walk to the bookcase where I angrily squashed the pamphlet between two tomes.

'I've already told you,' said Maria. 'He's a pet. And just look at him – so handsome!'

Whitefoot *was* handsome. He was entirely dusky grey apart from his left paw – a sock of purest white. As I watched him, the beast stretched out all his long legs at once.

'I thought you said he was an Irish hunting dog,' I replied drily. 'Yet I've never seen him give chase to so much as a mouse.'

This made Maria giggle. 'Nor does he pay any heed to the winter hares that venture into the gardens. Papa will be furious to see that he now lounges around like a king.'

But I was loath to engage in pleasantries with the girl when she had acted so sly. 'I'm going to see if Sylvia has heated water for me to take a bath,' I announced, making to walk to the door.

Maria eyed me suspiciously. She had never known me to seek out a bath unprompted. I always found them such a bother. All that undressing and redressing, getting my hair wet and soapy.

'You must snuff out the candles before you go,' directed Maria peevishly. 'I won't stay in here alone.'

Resigned, I turned on my heel and began extinguishing the numerous hot wicks with a metal snuffer. There were so many of them just in this one room – some set in sticks of solid silver, their drips cemented to petrified waterfalls, others spluttering wastefully within wide glass jars. Every one of them was fashioned from the finest beeswax.

Such an extravagance.

Back in the blackhouse, fatty tallow sticks were moulded from seal or whale blubber, salvaged when the great beasts beached themselves on to our shores. Even then, we could only use them sparsely – hardly ever during daylight hours, even though the inside of the blackhouse was always dark. But the burning of tallow sticks was not allowed anywhere in the merchant's house, not even by the servants in their own quarters. The merchant, it was said, could not abide their acrid smoke, their imitation stench of whatever animal's fat they'd been shaped from. Maria told me that he said tallow smelt like death itself.

And I too was guilty of adoring the smell of beeswax. I worried how I would cope with the coarse odours of island life when I returned home. When my trunk had been brought up, only a matter of hours after I'd been installed in my new room, I found its stench already unbearable. Maria was away taking a bath and so before the girl set eyes on it, I dragged it down the corridor, up a small flight of stairs and pushed it under the eaves of the roof. And that's where it would stay, until it was time for me to leave.

But I had to keep the island in my sights – for it was my home, and Artair was waiting for me.

I wandered to the sideboard under the guise of snuffing out the candles there but my intention was to look at the massive rectangular map hung on the wall above it.

Its title was *Theatrum Orbis Terrarum*, Latin for 'Theatre of the World' and it was beautifully etched out in black on to calfskin and filled out in places with gold and silver leaf. I hesitated before snuffing out the next candle.

I found the irregularly shaped island called Anglia sandwiched between the Atlantic and the North Sea. There were no borderlands marked in Anglia, nor even a separation of England from Scotland. Compared to the rest of the world, the island seemed insignificant. Off the top north-west tip of Anglia, several half-hearted blobs were painted marooned out in the Atlantic. I couldn't be sure if any of them represented St Kilda but reckoned that was the direction from which my journey here had taken me.

All these oceans and lands that I had not known existed. I had promised Artair that I would return with all this knowledge, and wondered if I should try and make a copy of the map.

'Remember that it is possible to sail around the entire world,' said Maria, seeing what I was looking at. 'That the left and right side of the map are joined by the Pacific Ocean.'

'Because it is round like a pebble,' I mumbled to

myself. Father had been right after all.

'Papa has sailed most of it, of course,' the girl went on. 'Even to the Americas. But he says that there is still so much to discover – forests no one has ever set eyes on, beasts that your mind could not even conjure up.'

My eyes were drawn across the Atlantic, to the newly discovered Americas where a sailing ship was being tossed by perilous waves, closely pursued by a tentacle-clad monster.

'Where does he trade?' I said, wondering what other dastardly creatures lay beneath that vast tract of ocean and shivering at the thought of having to journey back across the sea to my island. 'And what kinds of things?'

'Silks from China, silver from Russia, clocks from Bavaria.' Maria had risen from her desk and had gone to kneel by Whitefoot's cushion. 'But he has made his fortune – these days his travels are mapped by other intentions.'

'His pursuit for this *rare* ingredient?' I said, not able to stop the sarcasm leaking into my voice. The pursuits of this rich man were starting to annoy me – sailing the world on a wild goose chase, bringing back special gifts for his already spoilt daughter. The man sounded like he'd never done a hard day's work in his life.

But Maria did not reply. She was too intent on bothering the dog.

'And if he completes his potion, Maria, what will his *intentions* be then?'

Maria by now was stroking Whitefoot, but his ears were slicked back and his teeth bared in a low growl.

'When Papa has found what he is looking for, he will take me back to Italy, because it will be safe for us to do so – and also I hate it here,' said Maria. 'And Papa gets me anything that I want.'

'But how will he knows that it works? I mean, who will he test it on?' I said, puzzled. 'And what about the mineral spring? Does he not care that he will leave behind such a wondrous resource?'

But Maria was too busy with Whitefoot to reply. The dog, now risen up on long, shaky legs, was backed up tight against the panelling on the wall, a look of pure fear in his eyes. I hoped whatever the merchant's latest present to his daughter was, it was not another pet.

Plaustrell was expected home two days before Christmas and William was stationed at the posts. The boy was ordered to blow a hunting horn twice on the merchant's approach so that a welcome committee could be assembled in the entrance hall.

By then, the entire manor house was in full flow of Christmas preparation. The doorways and fireplaces had taken on the look of mystical forests, decked out with thick twists of green foliage, shiny spiked holly and cream-tipped ivy. The kitchens meanwhile fanned out continual fogs of spiced meats and sweet pastries, and barrels of French wine had been hauled up from the cellars.

Maria, being far too impatient to await the sounding of the horn, had us both sitting by the fireplace in the entrance hall from early morning.

Even Whitefoot was restless, pacing the tiled floor with his gangly limbs, only stopping occasionally to make a pool of slobber at the front door.

'I told you Papa would keep his promise to be here by Christmas.' Maria glowed as she perched on a barley-twist chair. I sat in silence, winding a loose thread from my gown around my thumb until the tip of it turned ghostly white.

'Please don't fret,' said Maria, sensing my trepidation. 'Papa really is the most wonderful, kind person. Really, you have nothing to fear.'

But I was about to meet the man who had gone to extremes to find his daughter a suitable companion. And now this companion would greet him wearing his dead wife's clothing. Wanting to appear grateful, I made sure that the pearl necklace he had given me was on full display.

Whitefoot's paws skittered around the hall, pans clanked in the kitchen, and in the quieter moments we heard the soft ticking of the hall clock. I snapped the thread around my finger, causing the blood to rush back to the tip, blooming crimson.

Then, suddenly, the hunting horn blew and before the echo of the two long blasts had died, Maria had joined the dog in running around the hall in a frenzy.

'He's here, he's here,' she cried, wild curls flying out behind her. 'Everyone take their places!'

Eugene, sweat-beaded, scuttled out from the library and picked up a handbell from the sideboard. He began to ring it feverishly.

Within seconds the whole staff had emerged from their respective doorways to muster in the hallway, straightening caps and dusting down aprons. The servant replaced the bell shakily before smoothing down his shirt and rearranging his knickerbockers above the knees.

Unable to wait for the pulling of the doorbell, Maria ordered that the front door be opened wide, letting in long blasts of icy air. Whitefoot exited through it like a bullet, barking madly as he disappeared into the trees.

Then the entire household waited stock-still, listening for the sound of hooves until, ultimately, an elegant man on a grey mare emerged from the copse of trees, closely pursued by the lolling dog.

'Papa! Papa!' screamed Maria, running out from the house.

The man on horseback was dressed top to toe in black and wore a wide-brimmed hat topped with a blue feather. What looked to be a fully grown wild boar was strapped across his knee.

Whilst still some distance away, he threw his legs to one side of his saddle and dismounted dramatically, tossing the pig like a sack of flour to the ground. The dog by now was wagging his tail madly at his feet and the man patted Whitefoot's head before ordering him to sit and stay exactly where he was. Miraculously, Whitefoot obeyed, leaving Plaustrell free to sprint off again and scoop up his daughter into his arms.

Sylvia was barely able to contain herself, hopping about from one stockinged leg to the other whilst several other maids gave out giddy gasps of delight.

I, on the other hand, had the sudden urge to burst out laughing! My nerves had bubbled over into a hysteria brought on by the spectacle and I took several deep breaths, trying to regain my composure.

The servants, however, did not care an ounce to keep their dignity and flung themselves, one by one, on to the floor as the merchant strode up the steps and through the open door, still carrying Maria, a squirming mass of curls, in his arms.

Aware I was the only member of staff now standing, I knelt awkwardly on one knee, which still left me a few feet higher than the rest of his sprawled-out servants.

But I could not tell if the merchant had acknowledged my presence or even looked in my direction, because his hat obscured the top half of his face. The only part that was visible was his cleanly shaven jaw.

Up close his velvet doublet was spliced through at the sleeves with shimmers of gold and his breeches (also black) were tied with purple ribbons halfway up his slim calves. His legs, that seemed to go on for ever, ended with a pointy pair of black boots.

Still carrying Maria, he stood before each servant, permitting them to rise and kiss a massive ringed gem on his left hand.

'*Padrone*,' they all murmured, sounding delirious as they each took their turn kissing the ring.

Finally, after biblically reviving all his servants, the merchant finally lowered Maria gently to the floor.

'And who do we have here?' he said in perfect Gaelic, turning on his heel towards me.

Although it was not the first time I had heard a male voice speak my language since leaving the island, it still felt strange and delicious to my ear. He pulled up the brim of his hat to reveal a slim, handsome face with eyes flecked the same brownish yellow as his daughter's.

At a wave of his hands, all the servants stood up and bowed backwards out of the hallway, leaving my kneeling self alone and exposed.

'This is Iseabail, Papa,' said Maria importantly, pushing her curls out of her eyes. 'Isn't she quite the thing?'

The merchant looked at me intently. He was younger than I had expected and his features were familiar. But of course he was: he looked just like Maria.

'Please . . . stand,' he said.

I did as he asked and Plaustrell approached, but instead of offering his ring he proceeded to circle me twice, his boots clicking across the tiled floor like chicken's feet. I didn't meet his gaze but I knew that all the time his eyes were upon me – or upon his wife's gown, at the very least.

'I had Sylvia adjust all of the clothes to the right size.'
Maria beamed like she was showing off a dressed doll.
'This purple gown suits the skin tone best.' Then Maria
said something else in Italian that was not meant for my
ears.

The merchant did not answer but his eyes flicked to
the pearl resting just above the neck of the dress. Then he
walked over to the sideboard purposefully and pulled off
his gloves, one finger at a time. 'Let's not talk about
people as if they were not present, Maria,' he said in
Gaelic, laying the gloves next to a vase. 'It's rude. And
shut that door, will you, before we all catch our deaths.'

Maria blushed furiously, the brightest of pinks. 'Of
course, Papa,' she said, flouncing over to the door where
she stood fuming on the threshold, looking out towards
the moor. 'Whitefoot, come in now, boy!' she shouted,
her voice cracking as she swallowed her tears. 'Come in
now, good dog.'

But the dog just remained sitting in the exact same
spot as he had been ordered to by Plaustrell, for once not
seeming to mind the cold. As usual, he had no intention
of doing what she asked.

'You naughty thing!' she screamed, stamping her foot.
'Come to your mistress immediately!'

But the dog just gave out a small yelp and lay down.

And it was not until her father's lips emitted a deep
low whistle that the great dog sprang to life.

'Well, you can't come in now!' said Maria, pushing the

door closed hard before the dog could reach the step. I caught a glimpse of William approaching on horseback, leading the merchant's grey mare off to the stables with the dead pig slung once again over its back before the door was slammed shut.

'Unfaithful mutt,' said Maria, leaning back against the metal handle. I was surprised at how disrespectful Maria was to her father, but all he did about it was to throw me a conspiratorial look of amusement.

'Did you notice that I brought you a boar?' said the merchant cheerfully. 'I shot it on my way here, for the Christmas table. I'll have Cook stuff it and make it look fine.'

'That's not my gift, is it? You promised me a gift,' sulked Maria, walking over and taking my hand. 'We are bored with everything in this house, aren't we, Iseabail. Now where is it?'

'All in good time,' said the merchant patiently. 'My wagons will arrive this evening from the ship and you will not be disappointed by your bounty. For now, I need to settle in, take a bath, get rid of these filthy clothes.' And with this he took off his hat, revealing hair that was so closely shaven that his olive brown skull shone through.

'Papa, your hair!' said Maria, dropping my hand and running to his side. He indulged her by bowing down so that she could rub the dark-brown fuzz. 'Why is it so short? It feels like a scrubbing brush.'

'Lice,' he said, standing back up straight and scratching his head at the memory. 'Had to cut the whole lot off.' As testament to this, the back of his neck was noticeably lighter, as if it had until recently been covered up by hair. 'The ship was full of the creatures. I made sure I shaved off *every* hair on my body rather than bring vermin back to my own house.'

With this personal revelation, he looked at me directly, causing my cheeks to burn up.

'What you need is a bath full of sage,' said Maria, happy again. 'And your clothes will be soaked in vinegar solution immediately.'

'That's my girl,' he said, ruffling Maria's hair fondly. He turned back to me. 'We'll talk later, Iseabail – but for now, I need to give instruction to my household. Christmas is tomorrow!' He glanced down at his daughter. 'We have so much to prepare.'

'Isn't Papa wonderful?' said Maria later in the library. We had just finished our daily instruction with Father Ronan and were sitting by the fire with our embroidery.

'I must say that you are most alike,' I said, putting down my sewing hoop. 'Both in looks and in . . . manner.' I had quickly noted the startling resemblance between father and daughter – the dark skin and flecked eyes, the tallness, the way they held themselves with the arrogance of nobility.

She shot me an arch glance. 'Papa has requested an audience with you,' she said, guiding her needle through the gauze and pulling up the thread. 'After he has eaten and finished giving instruction to the servants.'

Maria had spent a good hour or so alone with her father after he'd bathed, and I was nervous as to what they had been talking about. Whatever it was, she had returned to the library in a good mood.

'Oh,' I said. 'I look forward to that.'

'Don't expect it to be a long meeting,' said Maria imperiously. 'He has so much to organize before Christmas, you see, so you are the least of his concerns.'

'Sounds like Christmas is important to him,' I muttered, insulted that I was to be allowed so little time with the man who had summoned me all the way here.

'It is. There's sure to be a big celebration – and Papa's parties are always full of surprises,' said Maria, pausing, her needle suspended in the air. 'I wonder who he will choose this year as his Lord of Misrule!'

'His Lord of what?'

'Misrule,' she repeated. 'Every Christmas, it's traditional to choose a member of the household to be the Lord of Misrule . . . a kind of king for the day. The person gets to sit on a throne, and everyone must wait on them hand and foot! The Lord is allowed to order everyone around as he or she pleases – even me and Papa!'

'Good grief,' I said, trying to imagine such a spectacle.

'Well, whoever it is, it will be quite an event. So much food and wine and delicacies brought from afar. I do hope Papa has brought back sweet dates. Where was

I . . . ? Oh yes! And tonight is Christmas Eve, so there will be a special midnight Mass.'

'It is good to have your papa home,' I said, thinking of how the house had already taken on a whole new feel in the few hours since his arrival. Now there was an endless stream of Italian song echoing around the corridors as the servants went about their duties, though all of this conviviality brought forth a sharp string of memories from home. Of Eilidh singing as Mammy prepared stew, of Artair knocking at the door, a fresh basket of guga from the hunt strung across his strong shoulders. Although most of the apprehension I had of meeting the merchant had lifted, I hoped I would be brave enough to broach the subject of my return home at our meeting.

'Well, let's all make the most of him before his things arrive,' sighed Maria. 'Because then we'll not see hide nor hair. He'll lock himself in his workshop, slave to his scrolls and potions.'

'There is good news on his missing ingredient?' I asked stealthily. What she had said in the library about going back to Italy should the potion be a success had been troubling me. Did he think that if he packed up his house-hold to return to Italy, then I would go with them?

As usual, Maria sidestepped the question. 'I peeked up into his study earlier,' she said, 'and he's already scribbling away at yet another of his translations. I bet there are more manuscripts on board his wagons when they arrive tonight.'

'Translations – you mean he changes one language into another?'

'That's another of his obsessions – he believes he can find cures for every affliction in the world by deciphering ancient scrolls. Mark my words, he'll be locked in that tower before Christmas is over – take his meals in there, sleep in there too!'

'There is a bed – inside his tower room?' I said, surprised. I'd been trying to imagine what lay inside the circular walls of the tower ever since Maria told me what she had glimpsed in there.

'I suppose that there must be – not that he has any intention of letting anyone in to see it. I should stay away from there if I were you. Papa can become rather frightful if disturbed from his work.'

'And all this . . . for a cure for the plague?' My voice dropped to a whisper as a thought occurred to me. 'But why this obsession, when his wife is already dead?'

Maria's look darkened; her sewing hoop dropped from her fingers. It rolled away across the floor.

'I'm sorry—' I began. 'I didn't mean to—'

But her eyes had taken on that faraway look again, just like when she recalled her mother's death back in the arbour.

'Have you ever seen a dead body, Iseabail?' she asked slowly.

'Several,' I said awkwardly, relieved that my tongue slip had not upset her. 'Though none ravaged by plague.'

'Of what then?' said Maria, still staring ahead at nothing. 'What do the people of your island die from, Iseabail?'

'Lack of food, the cold,' I said, embarrassed by this fact. 'Some die from fevers. Most people do not live to see old age. Many do not live even to be children.' I picked up her sewing hoop and held it back out to her.

'And what would you say the main difference was?' asked Maria, not seeing what I was offering her. I leant forward to drop the ring into her lap instead, catching a waft of sickly perfume. 'Between a body that was dead – and one that was alive?'

I sat back in my seat and thought for a moment, not wanting to upset her further. Her question brought to mind the little baby that my mother had lost a few years ago. It had been born strong and looked to flourish, but then it had been taken suddenly by the eight-day sickness.

'Iseabail?' said Maria, now looking at me. Desperately seeking an answer.

'Movement,' I said evenly, thinking of how the dead baby had looked to be sleeping. 'There is movement in a live body, even if it is sick. A flicker of the eyelids, a rise of the chest. But a dead body . . . lies quite still.'

Once again, I feared that I might have pricked a painful memory of the girl's mother. But instead, it appeared that I had enraptured Maria for she was staring at me in a most peculiar way.

'I think that you are quite right,' she said, quite

captivated. 'A body that moves must surely be living.'

I breathed a sigh of relief for having said the right thing.

Just then, there was a knock on the door and Sylvia entered. She conveyed a message to Maria and I made out the word 'Padrone'.

'Papa will see you in his study now,' said Maria picking up her embroidery airily. 'But I'd hurry along if I were you . . . before he becomes distracted.'

The merchant was sitting in his study, a small annexe set just off from his bedchamber, hunched over his desk in a high-backed chair. I had thought it odd that I should walk through his sleeping quarters, but things were such in this household that I was rarely surprised any more. It was the first time I had been in his chamber since my illness and his four-poster was now neatly made up and the lion bed-curtains were drawn right back to the wall. A strong scent of sweet, burning spice filled the air.

'Almost done,' he said without turning, sensing my presence at the threshold. He continued scratching away with his quill on a piece of vellum whilst referring to a tatty parchment unrolled across the length of his desk.

Finally, the merchant waved with his free hand. 'Please come in, Iseabail, pull up a stool.'

I would have rather remained standing but instead I fetched a seat from a nook near the fireplace. I placed the warmed stool on the rug and sat down, noticing that the merchant appeared to be wearing a black silk scarf wrapped around his head.

With a loud sigh, the scribbling ended abruptly, his quill rattling into the glass jar. He stood up to face me. Following the passage of my eyes, he reached up to touch the strange head-garment.

'It's called a turban,' he said, striding to the window. 'Very fashionable these days in Europe – and more hygienic than a wig. The mice don't want to live in it for one thing.'

'Very good, sir,' was all I could think to say.

He stooped his tall frame to look out of the window. Fresh snow had begun to fall and tiny crests of it had collected along the leaded ridges in the glass. 'You'll be used to this dreich weather? Must be even worse out on that island of yours.'

'The snow isn't too bad there,' I shrugged. 'It's more the wind one has to worry about.'

'Nice and warm in this house though, heh?' he said, clipping over to the fireplace where he stood with his back to the dying flame. 'Everything you could ever want here – good food, wine, hot water.'

'Yes, you have been most generous with your accom-modation . . . and everything else,' I said, my hand subconsciously brushing my skirt.

'I'm glad nothing went to waste,' he said, his gaze falling on the sumptuous material.

'I am sorry about your wife,' I began.

'Oh yes,' he said absently. 'Seems such a long time ago now. That's why I built a house here: so that my daughter would be safe – and so that she can benefit from the waters.'

'Yes, sir,' I said, to show I was listening, though I was really figuring out how to bring up the subject of my return home. Then I noticed that his eyes were not fixed on the bodice of his wife's dress but on the necklace resting above it.

'I see you are still wearing the pearl,' he commented, his gaze not wavering.

'Yes, I love it,' I said, my fingers seeking out the smooth orb. And that was the truth. For as time had marched on in the house, the necklace felt like the only thing of worth that truly belonged to me. 'I have several sea-pearls back on the island – but this one seems special.'

'That is because it is no ordinary pearl,' he replied smiling. 'Indeed, it once belonged to a Persian princess.'

'Then why give it to me?' I said, quite dumbfounded.

'I gave orders that the chosen girl was to put it on,' explained the merchant. 'It was kind of a test.'

'A test?'

'Legend has it,' the merchant went on, quite seriously, 'that the stone is a reflector of the soul: if it remains white, then the wearer is a girl pure of heart.'

Caileag ghealchridheach. There was that phrase again.

'So, if I had put it on and it had changed colour – then you would have had your sailor toss me over the side?' I said, nervously.

'Maybe just taken you back to your shores,' laughed the merchant, tearing his eyes from the pearl. 'I'm not a monster, you know!'

'But what does it mean?' I said, looking down at the pearl, which looked exactly as it had the first time I had put it on. 'This *pure of heart?*'

'Well, I couldn't just choose any old girl as a companion for Maria,' he explained. 'She's a delicate thing – prone to bouts of weakness. I needed to find a good girl, some- one virtuous and kind. A girl that would be compatible.'

The merchant seemed quite certain about the abilities of the stone. I, however, was not convinced – either that the stone could change colour, or that anyone could be truly compatible with Maria.

'I take it that you have been advised to take the waters here?' said the merchant, changing the subject and marching back to the window sill where a large jug sat within a china basin.

'Yes, sir.'

'Good, good,' he said, pouring himself a glass tumbler

full of water. 'The water here is special, you see – it has the ability to heal. It is the only reason any rational man would build a house in these desolate borderlands.' He paused, then added softly, 'It truly could mean the difference between life and death for Maria.'

Although Maria had already told me this many times, I hadn't realized that the girl was so ill. That she *needed* to take the waters here.

'If you've been drinking it every day then I'm betting you're feeling quite invigorated,' he mused, putting the glass to his lips and sniffing the liquid. 'It certainly helps Maria with her malaise.'

I didn't have the courage to say that, if his daughter's malaise was temper, it was getting worse. Nor that since coming to the house I felt anything but invigorated. In truth, what with the oppressive temperature of the rooms, the rich food, the lack of hard work, I'd been rendered weighty and lethargic.

'That tree growing by the tower has done me a world of favours,' the merchant continued, gulping down the water in one.

I nodded again, remembering Maria telling of how the tree had made the purchase of the land possible because the locals believed it was cursed.

'Little do the villagers know that I planted it myself!'

'You did what?' I said, shocked back into listening properly. 'You planted the spiky tree that grows by the tower?'

'Indeed I did,' went on the merchant roguishly. 'You see, I'd heard about the miraculous spring that bubbles up here. From a contemporary in Padua. He said it had completely healed him of his gout. You do know what gout is?' The merchant paused whilst I confirmed that I did. 'Well, when Maria became sick, I travelled here and made the laird an offer for his land. And a very good offer it was too!'

'And he accepted?'

'Not exactly,' said the merchant, clearing his throat. 'Not long after, however,' he went on, 'the laird passed away, and under the guise of paying my respects I secretly planted the tree. Then I waited. Within weeks there were tales of the laird leaving a curse on the land – rumours spread around, of course, by my men. As further evidence of this hex, a strange tree sprouted up next to the laird's old tower – rumoured to have the Devil living in its trunk!'

'But how could it grow that quickly?' I asked, thinking of the massive tree. Maria had showed me how to count the rings in logs to know the age of the tree from which they came – but even trees with small trunks took many years to reach any girth.

'It's a fast-growing variety – at one point, it was growing a whole inch per day!' laughed the merchant as he poured another glass of water and offered it to me. 'Then I sealed the deal by adding those obelisks to the moor. Now what do you think of that?'

I took the glass from him, cradling it in my palms, not knowing what to think.

He smiled expectantly, his eyebrows arching up towards his ridiculous turban.

Reluctantly, I took a sip.

'Isn't it marvellous?' he said, returning to his seat, satisfied. 'If only my dear Rachel could have benefited from it too.'

'I hear that you are working on a cure for the plague,' I ventured, wiping the water's metallic residue from my lips discreetly. It was the first time I had heard the name of his wife.

'Isn't everyone these days?' he said, waving his hand at such trivia. 'But what makes me different is my ability with languages. If you can see across them, you can unlock the secrets of the world.' At this he turned and picked up the old scroll he'd been copying from as evidence, bidding that I move in for a closer look. 'There is so much more than mere plague cures out there waiting to be uncovered, Iseabail. Many secrets from the ancients that have been lost to time.'

The parchment on his desk was covered in unfamiliar marks that I did not recognize as letters.

'It's written partly in Greek, partly in Hebrew,' he explained. 'And I'm trying to translate it into Latin.'

'Hebrew?'

'It's a language of the Middle East. See – the characters have been written using the flat side of a cut reed.'

I tried to focus in on the sea of symbols but couldn't make out anything recognizable. 'But what does it say?'

'It's a spell,' he said, looking at me directly.

'More old superstitions?' I commented, surprised. I had thought the merchant to be a man of science, yet here he was talking about spells.

He merely smiled. 'The scroll claims it contains a cure for death itself.'

I glanced away, a little uncomfortable at the subject – surely this was nonsense? 'Your daughter has certainly inherited your talent for languages,' I said earnestly. 'She is already quite fluent in Gaelic and Latin – as well as Italian, of course.'

'She is certainly wise beyond her years,' said the merchant.

'I can hardly believe she is only seven years old,' I said brightly.

At this the merchant tensed.

'She has spent too much time in the company of adults, that's all,' he said tersely, rolling up his scroll and focusing back on me. 'But I'm afraid things have grown a little wild around here in my absence. That dog, for instance: letting the thing have the run of the house with all its fleas – I've banished it to the stables where it can be of use.'

Now this bit of news would not go down well. Losing Whitefoot to the stables to be looked after by 'the boy'! Not that the dog had ever cared for her but Maria would be unbearable when she found out.

'I doubt its ability for catching rats, sir.'

'The dog will provide some extra security for the stables. I have a new animal arriving – it is rather valuable.'

'Is it a horse?' I ventured, thinking that this must be Maria's gift. Though why he would fear theft from the villagers when no one ever came near the place was beyond me.

'No, it's something rather more exotic,' he said, tapping his nose. 'Now I really must be getting on with this scroll, I'm afraid.'

'Very well,' I said reluctantly.

'There is something else?' he asked when I did not move from the spot.

I had intended to ask about going home, but my tongue had turned to jelly inside my mouth. 'I wanted to ask,' I said finally, my knees twisting inwards. 'About the letter to my chief.'

'Oh,' said Plaustrell, his tone jaded. 'I thought that you would have more interesting things to ask me about. Like my sunken garden . . . or my book collection.'

'Well, those things are highly interesting, but—'

'I understand,' he said, holding up one hand. 'Go on then.'

It would seem that just like his daughter, the merchant could quickly sour.

'The letter?' he said impatiently. 'I *believe* you had a question about it?'

My courage slipped away. I didn't want to ask any more – not with the merchant in such a mood. 'Did you write it?' I blurted out finally. 'Just that the calligraphy . . . it was so beautiful.'

'Of course,' said Plaustrell, raising a thin eyebrow in amusement. 'I take great pleasure in my writing. Now you must leave me, Iseabail. Please find Maria. You girls enjoy your evening.'

Without further dismissal he stood up, turned his chair and picked up his quill.

And so I was left there by the glowing embers, blankly staring at the symbol of the lion emblazoned across the tiles above the fireplace. Had the merchant forgotten that I had come here on the condition that I could return home? Or now he had observed me, enjoying the comforts of his house, did he assume that I would never want to leave?

That night, the household took delivery of several wagonloads of wine, food and fine goods brought overland from the merchant's ship moored in North Berwick. The wagons, however, uncoupled their loads just beyond the posts and hardy ponies from the stables were used in convoy to pull them the rest of the way down to the house.

I wagered the wagon drivers had been relieved at not having to engage further with the merchant's domain. For I was beginning to see the fear that the mysterious Alexander Plaustrell could evoke. His flamboyant clothing, the obsession with dead languages, the foreign servants who never left his estate . . . The posts on the moors were just markers, a mere boundary to the strangeness of all that lay within.

'The first wagon should get to the house soon,' said Maria, pointing excitedly out into the night through the lattice of the upper gallery. In the distance, lanterns flickered across the moor like will-o'-the-wisps, the whinny of frightened delivery horses carried on the wind.

We were snuggled in quilts inside the bay of the window seat, eagerly watching the first transfer take place up at the posts. Although the night was moonless, the lanterns amplified to halos on the snowy ground, allowing us to easily follow their progress.

'Here it comes now,' I chimed in as the first of the deliveries was brought out through the trees, a swinging lantern guiding the pony's path. The glare of the lantern bleached out the rider's face but I assumed that it was William.

But the wagon passed by and circled to the left, around the house to the stables, leaving us none the wiser of what might be aboard.

I yawned widely. It was well into the early hours, midnight Mass already a distant memory.

By the time the third wagon emerged, I was ready for my bed but Maria had other ideas.

'I won't go until I see the last load,' she insisted, pulling the quilt around her tightly. The servants were bustling in and out of doorways in the hall down below by now. The kitchen maids would be staying up all night spinning sweetness into puddings, grinding spice into meats with their fresh batch of exotic foodstuffs.

Oranges and lemons, cinnamon and vanilla, rose-water and dates and sacks of sugar had arrived to replenish the depleted storeroom. Maria was particularly looking forward to a honeyed Italian bread, the shape and size, she claimed, of a small boulder. It was an act of great persuasion as the last wagon had trundled by to get her to bed.

'It's not fair,' she complained as I tucked her in. 'I want to stay up all night.'

But seconds later, she was sleeping soundly, leaving me wide awake, listening to the dulled cacophony emanating from the kitchens.

I swung my legs out of bed and felt my way along the wooden panels of the dark corridor back to the window seat. The quarter moon emerged from the clouds, striking the flat sides of the posts on the moor like they were lit from within. And my mind was drawn back to the island. To the last night I'd spent there, walking along the cliffs with Artair, looking at the moon, the endless stars. Back there the celebrations would be around the winter solstice, not Christmas. The islanders would kill the weaker sheep, for they would be unlikely to make it through the winter, and there would be a feast, a last sustenance before the hellish months running up to spring. I vowed that the day after Christmas I would ask the merchant about the promise of supplies – I prayed that they had been safely delivered. Then I would ask to go home.

The clock in the hallway below chimed two and I resigned myself to turning in. But then, I sensed a movement out across the ridge.

Approaching was another wagon.

On cue, not one but two steeds rode out from the back of the house and disappeared into the trees to meet it. The moon now afforded enough light to make out the identity of the figures of two men – one on a pony, the other on an elegant horse.

William and Plaustrell.

I didn't have to wait long for them to gallop up through the other side of the trees and on to the moor where the single wagon slowed to a halt. The wagon looked bigger than the ones that had arrived so far, its black silhouette revealing it carried a large, square crate.

Maria's present.

As the two parties converged on one another at the posts, I felt my neck grow pleasantly warm. Looking down, I observed the sheen of the pearl, fiercely catching the weak moonlight.

I pulled up the leather twine, dangling the stone before my face. The pearl hadn't changed colour but its whiteness seemed to shift like water was flowing beneath its lustrous surface.

I recalled something that my father had once said about the pearls I had found growing in clams at the beach. That because the tides were affected by the moon, so were the stones that grew within the sea. That they were connected. That they could not resist each other.

I was so mesmerized by the pearl that I did not witness the recoupling of the wagon. The next thing I knew, William's pony was leading it out from the trees towards the house, Plaustrell's horse riding closely at its side.

The procession passed by the house and turned towards the stables as I pressed my face against the window for a better view. By now the pearl was glowing and I was torn between watching it and following the progress of the wagon.

I pushed the pearl back under my nightgown and focused on the crate. It was too small to contain a horse and on closer inspection had a cage framing the wood, the moonlight glinting off the metal.

I figured that it was another pet for Maria. After all, Plaustrell had said that it was *exotic*. But what animal could be so precious that it needed locking away like this?

Forests no one has ever set eyes on, beasts that your mind could not even conjure up. That's what Maria had said when I asked about her father's travels.

Suddenly I yawned widely; I had to get some sleep. I began feeling my way back through the corridor only hoping that whatever was in the box was robust enough to cope with the affections of the girl. By the time I lay down beside Maria, the pearl had grown cold again against my chest. I fell into a deep sleep.

When Maria awoke on Christmas morning the first thing she did was sneak out to the stables to fetch Whitefoot, claiming that she simply could not enjoy the day if he was to be neglected. She came back covered in snow, dragging the great beast behind her.

'That accursed stable boy,' she steamed as we changed into our outfits for the day while Whitefoot pawed the door of our bedchamber, desperate to escape back outside. 'He had Whitefoot tethered outside the stables. The poor thing – it's a wonder he hasn't frozen to death.'

'He looks fine to me,' I said, trying not to breathe in as

I tied her hair up in a ribbon. Today her perfume was a special Christmas pomade concocted by Sylvia and she had certainly not been frugal in its appliance. 'Dogs are hardy beasts.'

I refrained from mentioning that I had seen a crate arriving last night and that Whitefoot was probably guarding her new pet in the stables.

Whitefoot did look fine, better in fact. Like he'd been given a purpose in life. I felt sorry for him being back in the confines of the house. The creature whined, desperate to be let back out.

'I swear that wretched boy has set him against me,' said Maria venomously as she clipped the lace on to my sleeves, and I fretted that the great dog would split the door in two. 'Just like he has done with Velvet.'

I was incredulous that she didn't realize that neither Whitefoot nor Velvet had ever cared for her in the first place.

'Is William invited to the feast today?' I enquired casually as she was fastening me into my dress. She had chosen for me a gaudy green gown that she said was most fitting for the celebrations. But my desire for the presence of the stable boy was not lost on the girl.

'Why do you keep asking about him?' she said peevishly, pulling the ribbon cords around the wrist too tight. 'Anyone would think that you were in love with him.'

'What do you mean?' I said, pulling my arm away and loosening the ribbon with my free hand. There was a friction mark where it had burnt into the skin just below my left wrist, skirting the scar where Eilidh had stabbed me. The friction mark faded within seconds leaving just the old scar, ugly and proud.

'I've seen how you look at him,' Maria went on, whilst I traced the scar with my finger, suddenly drawn back to the day Artair had balanced on the Maiden's Rock. 'Gawping like a cod-fish.'

'I do nothing of the sort,' I said, covering my wrist up again with my sleeve. How badly did I want to tell her that I was betrothed to Artair! That I would be returning home to him sometime soon. It took great resolve to bite my tongue. 'And I was merely asking if he would be joining the rest of the household. Now please, fasten me in more gently.'

'Well, stay still, will you?' said Maria, taking back my arm firmly. 'Or we'll miss out on all of the good bits.'

After dressing we descended the stair to a household already embroiled in euphoric chaos.

The first shock of the day was that the servants were all dressed as lords and ladies. I recognized several of the outfits on the women being paraded around, though I couldn't claim any of them really belonged to me.

'Don't they look ridiculous?' giggled Maria as I struggled to identify some of the wearers as they also wore heavy make-up.

Father Ronan was dressed in a servant's attire, but the red pantaloons were far too tight, making his stout legs look like sausages. Needless to say, he was already blind drunk.

'I wonder who Papa has in mind for Lord of Misrule,' snickered Maria as we helped ourselves to sweet orange loaves topped with cider-soaked figs. 'I do hope it's not the priest.'

Suddenly a horn sounded, and everyone pushed into the hall. There must have been twenty or so people packed in there, all jostling and elbowing for position. At the front of everyone, at the foot of the stairs stood William. He was dressed as himself in plain old breeches, his hair lit gold by a battalion of festive candles. In his hand was the curved lizard horn he'd used to summon the entire household. And like the rest of the servants, he looked tired, no doubt not getting to bed last night for attending to the merchant's newly arrived beast.

Our eyes met over the top of the crowd, but fearing more accusations from Maria I looked away quickly.

Then Sylvia busied herself to the front and William disappeared into the crowd.

'*Signore e signori*,' she said in a silly falsetto. She was wearing a red dress with an enormous ruff strangling her scraggy neck. '*Permettetemi di presentarvi il nostro Grande Spettacolo!*'

Three of the servants each took up an instrument – a flute, a harp and a drum and began to play a dramatic march.

'That means that Papa is coming!' Maria shouted over

the din into my ear. 'Just wait until you see!'

Everyone began to sing what I assumed to be an Italian carol as a tall spectre dressed in a multicoloured outfit appeared on the landing. As the figure began to descend the stair, its face was revealed to be a featureless mask.

Everyone began to clap voraciously as the spectre swept around the curve of the stair to begin his final descent into the hall. Of course, it was unmistakably the merchant but the crowd went berserk with the theatre of it all.

'*Benvenuti!*' cried Sylvia. '*Vi presento . . . Harlequin!*'

'Not Harlequin again,' said Maria, puffing out her cheeks with dissatisfaction. 'He wore that last year – I mean, he could have made more of an effort!'

The servants, it would seem, did not share her disappointment.

When the figure reached the last few steps, it halted dramatically, sending the musicians' instruments screeching to a halt. The mask stared out blankly across the hall.

A hush descended as Harlequin made to remove his mask. With a flourish it dropped clattering to the floor like a bird shot through the heart. And there he stood in all his glory: Alexander Plaustrell, the supposed master of this house, dressed head to toe as a court jester.

'*Signore e signori,*' began Plaustrell. Beneath his mask, he wore no make-up and his eyes looked red. Like he too had been up all night.

'I'll translate for you,' whispered Maria, craning up to my ear.

Her papa proceeded to address the entire household, thanking each of them for their unswerving loyalty in his absence especially in the face of the evils currently sweeping the country.

I tried to locate William again but Maria held on to my shoulder. She was now up on tiptoes, translating every word her father said directly into my ear.

'Now he's saying that we are safe here away from Venice,' she went on, her spittle finding my cheek. 'Here, we can all flourish, away from the clutches of death – though he feels he is close to finding a potion which will keep them all safe on their eventual return.'

This gave rise to further cheering, though all I could think was that if the Protestants came knocking right now, we would all be hung, drawn and quartered in the village square before sunrise.

Discreetly, I wiped my cheek, noticing that Maria's breath smelt bad.

'*E ora,*' said Plaustrell finally, smiling wildly.

'Here it comes!' squeaked Maria excitedly.

Sylvia moved to the front of the crowd and presented a cushion of scarlet velvet to her master, on top of which sat a silver crown. Plaustrell clomped down the remaining stairs and on to the black and white tiles, where he lifted the crown ceremonially from its cushion and Sylvia melted back into the crowd.

'I give you this year's . . . *Lord of Misrule*!' he said loudly and, very unexpectedly, in Gaelic.

But just then I spotted glimpses of ginger hair between the wigs and paraphernalia of the baying crowd. William emerged at the front holding a golden cage, partly draped in red cloth. It was a struggle for him to hold the cage aloft.

Whispering began amongst the crowd. What on earth was the master up to?

Suddenly Plaustrell stepped forward and whipped away the cover dramatically. A gasp circulated the room. Inside the cage sat a monkey. A monkey dressed in white frilly attire. I blinked. My stomach twisted. *Nell?* The monkey from the boat . . .

'Behold! Your Lord of Misrule!'

Plaustrell basked in the shocked silence whilst the monkey sat at the bottom of its cage crunching nuts.

After an uncomfortable pause, Plaustrell started laughing. 'Come, come,' he implored, leading the crowd into the Great Hall. 'There is nothing to fear – just a little joke, that's all. This year, there will be no Lord of Misrule. Instead, I beg you to enjoy the festivities with no other breathing down your neck.'

'Curse you, Papa!' piped up Maria, enraged. 'What a rotten trick!'

But a relieved cheer rose up as the cage was put down on the long table and the room filled up with chatter and laughter. I frowned as I watched Plaustrell fiddle with the catch of the cage. Once the door was open, the creature took her chance to flee.

Cries went up around the hall as the monkey swiped a toffee apple from a silver platter.

'I know that monkey,' I said, under my breath.

'Don't be stupid,' said Maria. 'How can you know a monkey?'

I frowned. She was right: how could I tell? It must be another creature of the same species. 'I mean, I know of a monkey – which looked just the same,' I explained, colouring slightly as Plaustrell returned to Maria's side. Looking closer now, I could see that the monkey was dressed as a baby.

'You see! Even a peasant from nowhere has seen a monkey before!' she told her father bitterly, not caring that she was insulting me. 'Is this my gift, Papa? If so, it is very disappointing.'

'Now now, Maria, she's not your main present. And I'm sure that you will find the little creature quite amusing,' said Plaustrell, stroking her hair as she buried her face in his chest. 'Why don't you think of a name for her?'

It was then that I noticed that the merchant was staring right at me. And although his eyes were rimmed red with fatigue, something sparked behind them. He held my gaze. I looked at the monkey, and back at him, my heart pounding. The sailor had been bearded, his hair long – and he had kept his eyes averted. His accent had been thick too, and his manner almost subservient. Out of context, he and Plaustrell were nothing alike . . . but now, with the creature cavorting over the dinner table . . .

I clasped my hand over my mouth.

Marcus Amanza.

No wonder I had thought his face familiar! And now it was so clear, especially as fresh whiskers darkened the lower half of his fine-boned jaw. Just as they had when he was dressed as a sailor. But why on earth . . .

Maria spun round to face me and I quickly rearranged my expression into something neutral, even as the world reeled around me.

'You name it, Iseabail.' she said impatiently. 'Quickly now, so we can get some cake.'

The merchant looked at me expectantly.

'How about Nell?' I said, not dropping my gaze.

And then the real celebrations began. By noon I could no longer stomach the self-replenishing mountains of food, nor the endless stream of outrageous party games. Plaustrell – *or 'Marcus Amanza'*, I thought bitterly – was nowhere to be seen and Maria was giddy with excitement, playing games with the servants. She assured me that her father would return before the day was done.

To suppress my shock, embarrassment and confusion about the merchant's revelation, I had drunk far more than my usual few glasses of ale throughout the day, indulging in French wine and the honey mead the priest had ordered from the priory.

The party went on all day, but as day turned to evening and yet another round of blind man's bluff was instigated, a wave of anger engulfed me; I could not bear it if the merchant returned to his party. How could I watch him parading around playing the fool after he had tricked me so cruelly? Was he my host, or my captor? Grabbing a fur cape, I fled out unseen through the back of the house.

I stumbled through the snow, inhaling deep breaths of cold air. How good it was to be out here, away from their drunken cheer.

My boots slipped on the icy steps down into the sunken garden, the silence soothing after the cacophony of the Great Hall. The snow started up again, but as there was no wind it fell softly from the grey sky, each flake taking an age to whirl noiselessly to the ground.

To my left loomed Plaustrell's tower, caked white like a candle and, next to it, the Devil's tree, looking just like an ordinary fir beneath its cape of snow. The world felt unsteady beneath my feet.

I raised my face, capturing a heap of refreshing flakes in my mouth, my mind speculating about winter storms besetting the islands. Were the men watching the shores desperate for the hope of supplies? Or had they never believed a word of the letter, meeting its demands in return for nothing more than being rid of the strange sailor?

What if they were to learn that that very same sailor was now my master? Would they be so keen to welcome me back knowing that I had spent a year under the influence of his household?

Of course, I would not even burden Artair with the merchant's dual identity. But this thought stung me deepest of all. I had never before withheld information from Artair – neither of us had kept secrets from each other. But now, would there always be a wedge between us? God, how I missed Artair – and my island home with all its certainties.

I rounded the corner past the buried sundial and took a right past the arbour so that I could negotiate a foot-path through the snow. Maria wouldn't miss me out here for an hour or so, especially as I hadn't proved the most willing of party guests.

However, as the path curved round the frozen twigs of a mulberry bush, I thought that I heard a sound. I pulled up my cap and listened.

At first there was nothing – just the occasional disem-bodied cheer from the party dulled behind the thick walls of the manor house. But as I tuned into the silence, my ears picked out the sound of snow falling. Imperceptible as one feather brushing another, a sensation quickly to slip from one's grasp.

I made to replace my cap, but then my ears detected something else. A faint cooing.

There was a dovecote built into the outer perimeter of

the kitchen garden where the birds were kept for game and eggs, though the doves themselves were free to come and go as they pleased. But just as I thought I'd fixed the source of the cooing, the tone of it became woeful. Now it reminded me more of the seals back at home, calling to each other out on the rocks.

But we were too far from the sea for seals and there was no wind on which such an unlikely call could be carried. And anyway, the strange sound seemed to be coming from the stables.

Aware that Whitefoot might be on duty, I stole behind a frozen hedge bordering the gardens where I might sneak a view. Suddenly I was excited at the prospect of seeing William. In the Great Hall I had been too wound up in myself to seek him out and hadn't even noticed when he had slipped out from the celebrations.

But as I approached the stable I began to think that I had imagined the noise, that it was just the frozen silence playing tricks on me. If I was to come across William now, what excuse would I give him for being outside of the stables alone?

I peeped out from behind the snow-moulded privet. The stables were in clear sight but although a light shone from within, the doors were fastened.

And there it was again. The noise. And it was definitely coming from the stables.

It struck me then that it might be the sound of a mare about to give birth, though Maria had not informed me that one was in such a situation. Then again, hadn't the merchant mentioned he'd bring back a creature that would be kept in the stables?

Nell's cage was only small – the monkey had no need for the large reinforced crate that I had witnessed being delivered last night. The crate had contained something else.

My teeth began to chatter now I was stationary and I longed to be let into the warm stables. So what if I could not have a conversation with William? I wanted to see him anyway. Wanted to see someone who wasn't deceitful Plaustrell, or his fickle daughter, or the servants who could understand nothing I said. Besides, maybe he would show me Maria's new pet.

I slipped out from behind the bush, the alcohol giving me bravado, but just as I did so, a noise pieced the air.

'Whhaarroooooooo!'

It was the bark of a dog. In seconds a great bulk was upon me, knocking me breathless to the ground. Whitefoot pinned my shoulders with his paws.

'It's me, it's me,' is all I could say, but then the hound's weight was suddenly lifted and someone had me beneath the arms, wrenching me to my feet.

It was William. With a gesture of one hand, he commanded Whitefoot to retreat. The dog slunk off back to his post, the stable door now gaping ajar. William put one finger to his lips, then pointed it towards the house.

'I was just taking a walk,' I said, unsure if he could

understand me. 'And now I'm completely soaked.'

It was true. Instead of falling into powdery snow that I could brush off, I had ended up in icy slush. The snow around the stables appeared to be melting.

'What's going on?' I said, my eyes drawn to the stable doors which, in his haste, William had left open. Through the gap could be gleaned several oil lanterns hung from the posts of the stalls, all blazing with light. One of the stalls was sealed off with a blanket. 'Has the merchant brought Maria a new horse?' I said, trying to see past him.

William shook his head.

'Please,' I said, laying a hand on his sleeve. 'I would very much like to see.'

William looked anxiously back towards the house. I could tell that he desperately wanted to close the stable doors.

I tightened the grip on his arm. 'Just a little look – and I'll leave you in peace. I promise.'

After one more anxious look across the gardens, he took my arm and led me straight into the stables.

In the main space of the paddock stood the steeds with which I was now familiar along with Velvet and the merchant's grey mare. But the animals seemed on edge, causing William to administer clicks from his tongue.

'What's wrong with them?' I asked, knowing this was how he communicated with the horses in the absence of a voice.

William pointed to the covered stall and made a cradle with his arms.

'So it is a foal,' I said, puzzled. 'But why are the other horses unsettled?'

William shook his head, for a moment looking unsure what to do next.

I took matters into my own hands. Striding over to the stall, I pulled back the cover.

'It can't be,' I said staring at the little animal straining madly at its tether in the corner as William tried to reseal the stall with the blanket. 'Maria's present is . . . a goat?'

The animal was small, creamy-white with a tufty beard beneath its chin. It had been harnessed with a leather hood covering its ears and shackled to the stall with a silver chain.

At this William burst out in a nervous, silent laugh, letting the blanket drop to the ground. I started laughing too, until tears sprung to my eyes.

'I can't believe that this is what he's got her,' I said, ecstatic, as the giggles faded. 'She's going to be so angry!'

For a moment we looked at each other, forgetting the goat, oblivious to the horses' nervous stamping on the hay-strewn floor.

But then the goat started up again with its odd, resonant bleat.

I crouched down and put my hand out. 'It makes an awful racket, though I suppose it is rather endearing.'

But William caught hold of my arm, shaking his head fiercely.

'Look, it's calming down,' I said. 'It's stopped its bleating.'

William watched carefully as the goat moved towards me. Its eyes shone bright in the light of the oil lamps. I let it lick my left wrist, where my silvery scar reminded me of Eilidh.

'It has a pretty purple tongue,' I observed now, knowing that William could understand every word that I said. 'Maybe Maria will be pleased with it after all.'

I felt delirious to be here talking to him alone. The first real company I'd had since leaving the island. At last, no one was manipulating me, or tricking me.

The goat's tongue was slightly rough and left my skin tingling both warm and cold. Just then Whitefoot started up again outside and William motioned with his head that I should go. But I found that I could not tear myself from the animal, for I had suddenly been overcome with a tremendous sense of well-being. A feeling of being enveloped in a warm cloud of air and the ground falling away. I felt set free, just for a moment, like I was back on the island, soft white sand pushing up through my toes, a cool sea breeze on my face.

Impatient, William grabbed my arm and pulled me away – and I literally fell back to earth.

Suddenly I was jealous that this animal belonged to Maria.

'What if the goat doesn't like her?' I said, getting back to my feet and dusting the hay off my skirt. I was still in a daze and the goat's lick had left my hand with the most pleasant feeling. 'Will the merchant still let her keep it?'

William shook his head like he didn't know and led me to the door.

'I feel sorry for the poor little thing now,' I said. 'I mean, animals hate Maria.'

Then, feeling quite overcome with emotion from the wine, the laughter and the strange goat, I stood on my tiptoes and planted a kiss on William's cheek. 'For Christmas!' I explained. 'And please tell me I can come back and visit the goat tomorrow.'

William nodded – and blushed.

But once we were outside there was the sound of a door slamming and Whitefoot sniffed the air again sharply. He hurried out into the night. Someone was coming.

William's translucent skin turned even paler, a blue vein pulsing across his temple.

'Why are you so afraid?' I asked. 'Is the goat such a secret?'

William pushed me gently away into the darkness and motioned me to hurry. Hearing footsteps crunching throw the snow, I ducked behind a bush nearby, glimpsing William's red hair as he pulled the stable doors shut.

Whitefoot remained on his feet, still agitated. A figure strode forward from the shadows – it was Plaustrell, still dressed in his jester's outfit and heading for the stables. He was coming from the direction of the tower, not the main house.

I noticed that his footfall changed as he crossed on to the snow melt. He patted Whitefoot on the head as he passed, the dog trotting after him obediently. The stable doors opened and shut.

I sat for a few moments in the silence, trying to figure out why the snow had only melted around the stables. I didn't want to return to the house just yet . . . and with Plaustrell accounted for with William, a sudden urge took hold of me. My feet carried me towards another forbidden place.

The tower loomed large in front of me. But the path to the door was now churned up and trodden, the lid of snow around the door cracked. A curl of smoke snaked from a pipe chimney poking out from the curved brick wall. Plaustrell must have reinstalled himself – I was lucky not to have been caught in the stables. My heart beat fast in my chest, high on the danger of it all.

After one tentative breath turned to steam in the cold air, I crossed the trodden snow up to the tower and pushed down the metal handle of the door.

The hinge opened inwards, spinning me into a room I wasn't really expecting. Although the space was circular, it was not the suspected height. Instead, the chamber had been made snug by a low, beamed ceiling. Only the lowest of the windows was visible, a clay oil lamp balanced on its stucco ledge, its flickering duplicated in the clover-leaf of glass. Dotted around the room, stout beeswax candles danced in glass jars, their shadows liberated around the bare stone walls. And again, there was that spicy aroma, the same one that had filled the merchant's bedchamber last night, heady wafts of foreign perfumes that I now recognized from the Christmas feast – nutmeg, cinnamon, vanilla, orange: spices burning thousands of miles from their native Far East.

I shut the door to prevent intrusions of snow, wiping my feet on the straw mat, all the while my eyes adjusting to the shapes in the dimness – a four-poster bed, unmade and rumpled, a throne-like chair set by a brick fireplace, a trestle strewn with bowls. I walked over to these things in turn, my damp boots slipping over the mosaic floor, its opulence entirely out of place with the otherwise rustic decor.

I swiped a finger along the trestle, leaving a trail through a coating of dust, a testament to none of the servants being allowed in here. I wasn't allowed in here either, but despite the knowledge that Plaustrell could very well have been finished in the stables, I made my way over to the fire to warm my hands.

Now I was in here, in the merchant's forbidden tower, I felt disappointed. Where were these curiosities Maria spoke of? These jars filled with the grotesque? The stash of tattered scrolls rescued from the obscurity of millennia?

The tower was just another room, inferior to those within the house, with a scattering of furnishings. It was a haven from which the master could escape the household, evade the clutches of his demanding child. Nothing more.

My hands warmed, I made to leave. There was no point in getting caught in here – all for the sake of nothing. But then something caught my eye. A leather-bound book. It was set atop a low table nestled by the side of the throne-chair. So the merchant did keep more books in here after all.

I knelt beside the table and flipped open the cover, revealing a highly decorated title page. But so wrought was the drawing, with branches woven intricately with hanging fruits and songbirds that at first, I could not make out the name of the book. Then, as my eyes adjusted, the title gradually emerged: *Compendium Bestiarum*, a compendium of beasts.

My rudimentary Latin served me well in working out a translation to the title and I was convinced that there was no other book like it in the house. I turned over the first pages carefully, my eyes struggling to focus on the Latin text beneath the intricate artwork. Each page was embossed in both gold and silver leaf, the text inked in either black or burgundy, and featured illustrations of magnificent beasts.

The first pages were given over to Adam, the first man created by God, and his naming of the beasts, my poor

Latin allowing me to string together a few words and phrases. I had flipped over several more pages before noting a piece of red silk protruding from the upper edge of the book. I prised open the pages which it marked.

And there was a painting of a young maiden sitting on a rock in a woodland clearing. She was painted piously, with flowing blonde hair tumbling out over sapphire robes. Across her knee stretched a white animal with a tail that ended in a fluff, not unlike the stuffed lion's in the merchant's workshop. From its forehead extended a single long twisted horn.

I tried to figure out the writing but there was a scuffling from outside the door. I shut the book up quickly and replaced it on the table.

In a panic, I sought a place to hide in the room. There were no corners, of course, and the tower was so sparsely furnished that my choice of hiding place was limited. Quickly I piled into the merchant's messy bed, pulling a sheepskin cover up over my head.

I lay there shaking, hardly daring to take a breath. After a few minutes, however, with no further noises occurring, I cautiously raised the covers. The door had not been opened and I looked around frantically for another means of escape though I knew fine well, from daily walks around the tower, that there was only one means of exit.

But I had missed something. For in the darkest part of the room, furthest away from the window, a thin ladder led up from the ground floor through a hole into the low ceiling. The lack of illumination in that area had caused it to remain hidden until my desperate eyes had sought it out: the entrance to the merchant's workshop.

Up that ladder must be the place where he kept his secrets and treasures, where he mixed up his medicines using the rarest ingredients. But what use was this information to me now? If I made it up the ladder unseen, I would be trapped when the merchant entered through the ground floor. My best bet was to remain here, in the safety of the bed then, when the merchant opened the door, I would lie as still as a hunted fox until he ascended to his workshop. At that point, I could slip undetected out of the door and make my way back through the gardens, back to the festivities of the house.

I lay there in the four-poster bed, enveloped in the sheepskin as the residual alcohol took away my last ounce of energy. How I wished I was back home, tucked into my simple bunk in the blackhouse. I'd be cold and most probably hungry, but at least I'd be safe, there with my own kind. A sharp thorn pierced my heart as I ran through the events of the afternoon – Plaustrell's deception revealed, the drinking, the games, the strange goat. And how could I have just kissed the stable boy? I suppressed a groan of mingled guilt and embarrassment. I thought of Artair, about returning home to be his wife. I prayed that his eye was also not being turned by another in my absence. Perhaps by my beautiful sister Eilidh?

I stroked my scar, thinking of Eilidh singing one of her sweet island lullabies. Despite her fierce nature, she had the voice of an angel. And even though she had stabbed me the night of my betrothal, our dispute had been short-lived.

I thought of her face as I'd boarded the boat. She had not wanted me to leave. She would be suffering without me as I was now without her. Despite our differences, we were close. We had always had one another.

I awoke suddenly in the dark and sat bolt upright, freeing myself from a dream in which I had become trapped in the merchant's tower.

Then I remembered that I *was* in the merchant's tower!

I looked around me. Most of the candles had gone out by now but a few remained, flickering across the patterns of the bed quilt. I couldn't believe that I had fallen asleep here. And the worse thing was that someone was lying beside me – somebody lying very still.

Suddenly the person sat up. 'Are you having a bad dream?' said a sickly sweet voice.

But I was too terrified to reply, recoiling in horror at the being that had sprung up next to me, its raw, pitted nose glistening in the candlelight.

The face sat almost featureless above a stained nightgown, its skin bursting with pustules and sores. A slab of rotten meat with luxuriant hair, scabs leaking eggy pus on to the pillows.

'Iseabail,' said the thing, its mouth just a gaping hole.

But I could not find my voice, only a silent scream.

'Wake up!' said the voice. But now I was aware that my eyes were closed and that I was being shaken awake. 'It's me, it's Maria!'

I dared to open my eyes, finding myself back in my own bedchamber. The girl was leaning over me.

'I think that you might have been having a nightmare!' she declared. The curtains at the window hadn't been properly drawn and the blue light of dawn cast across her face.

Smooth skin. Normal. Though her perfume was just as ghastly as usual. It took me several moments to believe that I really was safe, back in my own bedchamber beside the girl, not inside the tower waking up beside a hideous ghoul.

'I'm all right,' I said, sliding back down on to the pillow, my forehead moist with sweat from the dream. 'I had a night terror, that's all. Sorry if I woke you.'

'When did you come to bed?' asked Maria, lying back down and tugging on the quilt. 'You went missing at dusk and you still weren't back when it was time to go to turn in.'

'Late,' I said, trying to remember myself. 'Very late. I . . . I fell asleep in the library . . . too much wine, you see. Then later when it was dark again, I came up here.'

But the truth was that I had no idea of how I came to be lying in my own bed after the day's events, wearing only my undergarments.

I lay back down, head throbbing, my throat as dry as sticks.

'Well, I hope your head hurts,' said Maria, almost back to sleep again. 'Leaving me like that – in the middle of Christmas day!'

It did hurt and I swore never to drink again, blaming the wine for conjuring up all of last night's strangeness. Had I even gone for a walk in the grounds on Christmas day or had I merely fallen into a stupor somewhere in the house and dreamt the whole thing?

Yet . . . the memory of my journey through the garden was too real to be a dream. The snow, the cooing sound, the joy of the baby goat, the kiss I'd planted on William's cheek. How could they be figments of my imagination?

'Did you get your present, Maria?' I asked the girl. But she was already back to sleep, snoring gently.

I swung my legs out of bed, desperate for a drink. A jug of freshly drawn water was usually kept on the window sill, so I stumbled about feeling for the edge of the dresser. Instead, I bumped straight into a chair, the back of which was covered in a velvety cloth. I recognized it immediately, even in the dimness, as my Christmas dress.

I smoothed it down feeling sick, wondering who might have laid it there after they'd relieved me of it, then left me to sleep. My hand brushed the hem. It was dripping wet, testament of my walk through the snowy gardens. But hadn't I ended up in the tower?

After swigging straight from the jug I lay back down, listening to the wind howling across the moor, the residue of the water clinging to my parched lips. The water in the jug was replaced fresh every day, but even a few hours of settlement rendered it stale-tasting, gritty.

My head throbbed. How on earth was I going to explain all of this? The merchant must have found me trespassing in his tower – in his very own bed, before dragging me back up to my own chamber.

Oh, the shame of it, the humiliation! Would he be angry? Deeply offended? Would he turn me out of his house into the snow? I prayed that he had already retreated to his tower and that he was so wrapped up in his precious work that he might completely forget what had taken place last night.

Maria woke me again just before noon to summon me to Mass. She had picked me out a rather sombre outfit, a white blouse with a plain black skirt. The snow-wet dress had disappeared from the chair, presumably taken to the laundry.

The girl was in a foul mood, probably because she had still not received her real present. I wondered why the merchant was keeping it from her in the stables.

After Mass, a feast of sorts had been assembled in the Great Hall. The food was half-hearted compared to yesterday, the table of desserts and jellies rather sad and flaccid.

After we had eaten Maria announced that her papa requested my presence in the library.

'Isn't he busy in his tower?' I asked, alarmed at the prospect.

'I imagine so,' said Maria sulkily. 'And he must have taken that stinking monkey with him – but he won't let *you* in there, that's why he is using the library. Please ask one of the servants for more logs for the fire on your way there.'

I swallowed a lump of vomit rising in my throat. The thought of apologizing to the merchant for carrying me through the house back to bed made me faint. I'd almost forgotten to be angry with him about his Marcus Amanza charade.

After knocking, I entered the library where I found Plaustrell standing with his back to me. He was dressed smartly in black again, his arms folded behind him so that the puffed sleeves of his jacket rested on his rump. He was leaning over the sideboard, looking at the map.

I stepped gingerly into the library and stood by the door.

'How is your head this morning?' he enquired, without taking his eyes off the map.

'It is well, sir,' I replied.

'Don't lie, Iseabail, it doesn't suit you,' he said, turning to face me. 'But it was Christmas, so don't worry about it. Now if you would be so good as to let me see your hands.'

'My hands, sir?'

'I want to check how clean they are,' he said, taking a step towards me. My legs turned to jelly as I walked to meet him halfway across the room.

I offered out my arms and he took my hands, first examining the front of them, then the back. 'And you do not feel unwell this morning?'

'A little, I suppose,' I concurred, not daring to fabricate the truth again. 'My head throbs.'

'That will be the wine,' sniffed the merchant, flipping my hands to examine my palms again. 'French stuff, you see – it can be rather strong.'

'Yes, sir,' I said, also looking down at my hands, puzzled at his intense interest though I was glad he hadn't confronted me about the tower.

But then I snatched them back.

'My God, where is it?' I said, turning my left hand back and forth.

'Where is what?' asked the merchant, genuinely bemused.

'My scar,' I went on. 'I had a scar . . . on my left hand. From an injury – it's gone!'

'Show me!' said the merchant, excited now. 'Where was this wound of yours?'

'Right here,' I said, tracing over the place where the scar should have been with my right forefinger. 'This is where my sister . . .'

The merchant looked at me quizzically.

'You see, sir,' I explained. 'About a year ago. We had a fight and, well, she . . .'

'Must have been quite a fight,' said the merchant, amused. 'I noticed that she was a fiery one – when she saw you off on the boat. By the way, I didn't completely make up my incognito that day – my middle names are, in fact, Marcus Amanza.'

But I wasn't thinking of Eilidh any more, nor the merchant's sailor disguise. I was thinking of the wound. Initially, it had knitted together fine because Mammy had wrapped it in a seaweed poultice, but it hadn't healed completely, and looked like it never would. But now it was gone.

When I looked up at the merchant, he was staring at me intently. 'You're serious about this, aren't you?' he said as I continued to twist and turn my wrist in a desperate search for my scar. I even checked my other hand in case I had forgotten which wrist it had been on.

'Might have been the water,' mumbled the merchant almost to himself. 'I told you that it has healing properties.'

'But it was there only yesterday,' I protested.

The merchant walked over to the settee and sat down heavily, his forehead wrinkled as if he was trying to figure something out.

As I was myself. I remembered looking at the scar in the stables last night, that fold of puckered skin that served as my constant reminder of home. I used to think it ugly, but now realized how much it meant to me.

'I'm sorry about last night, Iseabail,' said the merchant after a time, his eyes browsing my hand again. 'It's my responsibility to look out for your welfare. Especially after bringing you all the way here. I should have reminded the servants to show you how to water down that wine.'

I blinked at the change of subject, suddenly angry that he thought the disappearance of a scar so trivial. 'I want to go home,' I blurted out. 'As soon as possible . . . when the seas are safe enough to pass?'

The merchant's eyes widened at my outburst and he blew out his cheeks in surprise. Then, sighing heavily, he folded his arms and leant back against the red silk of the settee. 'What do you think is waiting for you back there on that island, Iseabail? Something that you cannot find here?'

'Really, I am most grateful for everything you have given me,' I began, struggling to keep my emotions in check. 'But – I am betrothed to be married – as you well know.'

'You return for . . . a husband?' said the merchant, putting a finger to his lips in false contemplation.

I nodded, furiously. I had told him my intentions to return that day on the boat. And hadn't he witnessed with his own eyes Artair's emotional goodbye?

'Troublesome creatures, don't you think?' he said, his tone mocking. 'You would rather forgo an education to wait hand and foot on an illiterate man, risk your precious young life to bear his children?'

'But things will not be like that,' I said valiantly, affronted that he had referred to Artair in this way. 'Artair and I have discussed it. One day we will rule the islands together. As man and wife. As equals!'

The merchant digested this calmly before clearing his throat. 'Well, if childbirth doesn't kill you, then you'll be ground down by hard toil. An old hag by the time you are thirty,' he sneered, ignoring my declaration. 'I really thought that a mind as agile as yours would have been opened up to other possibilities by now. And Father Ronan has led me to believe that you are quite the scholar.'

'Returning to marry Artair is my destiny,' I went on, determined, though my bottom lip started to tremble. 'I don't belong in this house and the longer I stay here, the less I remember who I really am.' I looked down at my smooth wrist and remembered how I'd so easily kissed William last night. My tears, refusing to be contained any more, pushed hotly out from my lower lids and rolled down my cheeks. But I did not dry them. I wanted Plaustrell to see how I was suffering. Wanted to remind him of the promises he had made.

But the merchant busied himself with plucking bits of fluff from the bolster of the settee.

'The main reason I summoned you here today was to tell you that the supplies I promised your chief have left the port,' he said sulkily. 'Weather permitting they will be with your people in a matter of days.'

At this I perked up. 'Thank you, sir,' I said, finally wiping my tears. This news was so unexpected, so welcome. Whatever happened now, sending me here had not been entirely pointless.

'I apologize if I spoke out of turn just then sir, it's just . . .'

The merchant stood stiffly and held up his hand to stop me speaking.

'You know, it doesn't seem to matter how much I give you Iseabail,' he tutted, walking over to the bookcase. 'You never seem satisfied.'

'Sir?' I began, puzzled.

'I mean, look at all these fine volumes you now have at your disposal.' He plucked a small book from the shelf. 'And yet you insist on rifling around in private rooms in the pursuit of more?' At this he swivelled on his heel to look at me directly.

'I'm so sorry,' I said, beginning to tremble as I realized where his conversation was now heading.

'And tell me, Iseabail – after you'd finished with my fireside read, did sheer nerve carry you up the ladder?'

'No, sir, I swear!'

There was a moment of silence.

'Pity for you,' said the merchant, replacing the book.

Then he turned to me but now he was smiling. 'The upper reaches of my tower contain some quite marvellous things,' he beamed. 'Maybe I can show you sometime?'

'Yes,' I mumbled, wary at his change of mood.

'Though my daughter will be less than pleased if she knew you were to be granted access to my treasures,' he mused. 'Let me think of a diversion for her.'

Just then, there was a knock at the door and at Plaustrell's command, Sylvia stepped inside. The maid relayed a message in Italian. Even after my studies in Latin, which Father Ronan told me was not so different, I struggled to make much sense of the language.

'Now, if you will excuse me, Iseabail,' said the merchant genially, 'I must attend to my household. I'll send a distraction for Maria – a signal for you to come to the tower . . . when I find a convenient time.'

And there he left me alone on the threshold of the library, looking out into the glorious chequered entrance hall. The merchant's conversation had left me quite adrift. On the one hand he had honoured the winter supplies but, as I now realized, had evaded the question about my eventual return home, sidestepped it lightly with an invite to his fantastical workshop. And I had let him away with it, lapping up his latest offer like a grateful dog.

Walking out over the black and white tiles, I caught sight of myself in the hall mirror. Where was Iseabail McCleod, that fiery, barefoot girl who'd stood right here not so long ago having dragged her rough trunk across the snowy moor? A staunch, dutiful girl with full intention to return to her island, to her betrothed? Now there was only a gentlewoman, cloaked in the finest silks, cheeks plump with good living. My reflection looked back at me, genteel, stately – bearing no outward trace of my rough island self. And now the scar, one of my trusty reminders of my old life, had disappeared too.

I stepped closer to the mirror, hoping to see something of the old Iseabail. But other than a faint resemblance to my sister, there was so little left. The merchant's house, it was erasing me.

15

Two days later the *Beast Compendium* materialized on Maria's writing desk.

She read out the accompanying note excitedly:

Dearest Maria – please accept my apology for the delay with your gift. It got lost in the melee of Christmas deliveries.

'Finally, my present!' said Maria, picking it up greedily. She held it tight to her chest as I approached. 'I hope for Papa's sake it is as special as he claimed,' she said imperiously. 'Shall we take a look?'

I'd been awaiting the merchant's clandestine invitation ever since our meeting in the library. But now I was confused. If this was the gift that Maria had been expecting, then what was the animal in the stables for?

Also, the gift's arrival was the merchant's distraction, a mechanism to give me a chance of escape. Maria, however, was not letting me out of her sights.

'Maybe you should read it first,' I said, stepping away as if heading for the door. 'It's your present, after all.'

But this only fuelled her. It seemed to me that she was quicker than ever to anger these days. 'You do not wish to see it?' she said scornfully. 'This beautiful book that you have surely never laid eyes on?'

Defeated, I moved back over to the desk. I couldn't risk raising her suspicions that I had indeed seen the book before. I would need to think of another plan.

She placed the book importantly on the table and I noted that the red ribbon marker was still present.

She prised the book open with the ribbon. And there sat the maiden again in her woodland clearing, the one-horned creature draped across her knee.

'A unicornis!' Maria cried, following the text with one finger. '*A beast stronger than a lion with a horn that can cure any poison.*'

Then she looked at me directly.

'Only tameable by a maiden pure of heart,' she said with a strange smile.

'Let me see that,' I said, attempting to see the page that I had only glimpsed in the tower. 'What do you mean, *pure of heart*?'

But Maria pulled the compendium away from me.

'How dare you touch it,' she said. 'I'll say when you can look at it. Now why don't you just go – leave me alone!'

'Very well,' I conceded.

Leaving Maria to her book, I went off to the tower, though I couldn't help thinking about the girl in the picture and the appearance of that phrase again: pure of heart.

It was just after ten in the morning and the wind was howling around the hillock, though no further snow had fallen. I pulled my cap further over my ears and made ready to walk up the steps.

'Iseabail!'

I turned to see Father Ronan making his way up from the sunken garden. It was rather early to see him up and about.

'Where on earth do you think you are going?' he said, surprised to come across me too.

'The merchant has asked to see me,' I replied.

'And he's asked to meet you here?'

I nodded, wanting him just to go away. Despite my misgivings about how eagerly I'd accepted his invitation, I was curious to see the upper part of the tower and I worried Plaustrell would change his mind if I was late.

'I've been trying to work out what he's been up to in there,' the priest said, looking up at the line of clover-leaf windows disdainfully. 'Whatever it is, I'm not sure it's God's work.'

'But isn't the merchant a man of faith?'

Father Ronan seemed not to notice my question. 'There's something strange going on,' he added quietly. 'The snow around the stables, why – it's all gone.'

The ground under out feet was still frozen hard and covered in snow. 'Is that so?' I said, not really believing him and desperate to get to the tower. 'It's probably just where the sun strikes and melts it.' Then again, hadn't I fallen into a pile of slush near the stables when Whitefoot had leapt on me last night . . .

'Just be careful, child,' he said, shaking his head. 'Keep God close to your heart.' And he stumbled off in the direction of the house.

His words had a strange echo and I remembered that Innes Ferguson had said the same thing to me as I embarked on my voyage to the mainland. I shivered, suddenly full of doubt.

I waited until the priest was completely out of sight and then, shaking off my misgivings, ran up the steps to the door of the tower. Then I knocked and waited, my heart pounding; at last I was to see all those wonders that Maria had spoken of.

The door opened a crack. 'Ah, there you are,' said Plaustrell, opening it fully. 'Please come in, Iseabail. I thought sending Maria her gift would afford you a few hours' peace. I have to admit to holding on to it for a little while.'

I was ushered into the low-ceilinged room which looked much as it had on the evening of Christmas day except there was more daylight entering through the clover-leaf window.

'Let me stoke the fire,' said Plaustrell, directing me to sit in the throne-chair.

The merchant was wearing simple clothes again and appeared far more relaxed in the tower than he was in the confines of his grand house. He moved off gracefully towards the back of the room, returning moments later holding a tray set with two small cups and a strange kind of metal pot, which he put on an octagonal veneered table beside the fireplace. It was the table on which the *Beast Compendium* had sat. My heart sank. Maybe he wasn't going to show me to the second floor at all.

I sat by the fireplace, thankful it only held a small grate. The library was stifling in comparison.

'Beautiful, isn't it,' said Plaustrell as he slid the tray upon the table, hiding the pearly geometric design. 'Inlaid with animal bone, all the way from India.'

'You own so many beautiful things,' I said, arranging my skirt about the chair nervously. 'Many that until a few months ago I never would have believed existed.'

'And yet?' said the merchant, without looking up from the tray.

I took a deep breath. 'I must tell you that I miss my old life.'

I worried about the effect of this revelation, but he calmly pulled up a three-legged stool and sat down on it, indicating that I should remain in the throne-chair.

'It is not always easy,' he mused, arranging the tiny handleless cups around the metal pot, which I noticed had a curved spout and a handle. The cups were painted intricately with dragons and scaly fish, a style that featured throughout his house, a style that I had learnt was known as 'oriental'. He reached over to retrieve the kettle from the stove and poured hot water into the pot. 'This journey from rags to riches. You may be surprised to learn that I too came from far humbler beginnings.'

'You mean that your father before you was not also a merchant?' I asked, intrigued, hardly noticing that he was once again avoiding the subject of my return home.

'No, very far from it,' he continued, inching his stool closer to the squat table. 'He never left the village where he was born. Died there too, after a hard and thankless life.'

I noticed that he hadn't shaved again and the stubble had thickened considerably over his lower jaw.

'His trade, if you can believe it, was that of a simple woodcarver. And I was his apprentice, set to follow in his footsteps.'

'But then how did you come to all of this?' I asked, feeling more at ease because of Plaustrell's revelation about his humble beginnings.

'I ran away to Venice when I was twelve, taken in by a priest who had me schooled. Nobody could believe how hungry I was for knowledge, how quickly I learnt languages.'

'Did you ever return to your own village?'

'No, never,' said the merchant, picking up the metal pot, its spout emitting a trail of steam. 'I went to university,' he said, changing the subject. 'Where I studied anatomy, though languages will always be my true passion.'

I looked at him quizzically.

'Anatomy is the study of the human body,' he went on, pouring the bronze liquid into the cups. 'And Padua is the most forward-thinking of the universities.'

'But then how did you come to be a merchant?' I said, watching the ground leaves collecting in a minute sieve.

'A means to an end,' laughed the merchant. 'I needed a way of making money once I left the monastery – to fund my work. But let's focus on the task at hand. This drink I'm serving is called tea and the Chinese have a whole ceremony attached to it.'

I took the scalding cup from his hands and inhaled the grassy aroma. It was uplifting, green and good.

'They use it for contemplation, and . . . to say thank you,' he said, taking a cup himself. 'And it is you that I would like to show my gratitude – for being such a faithful companion to my daughter.'

'You are too kind,' I mumbled, embarrassed now about my ungrateful outburst in the library yesterday. He looked up at me with gold-flecked eyes, his stool far lower than the throne-chair. We finished our tea in silence.

'Well, I have to say that you take your tea with the elegance of a Chinese noble,' he said, wiping his lips and standing. He picked up the stool and placed it back against the stone wall. 'It might be harder than you think to return to your simple life.'

'Really, I am just my same old self,' I said, flustered by the veiled compliment. 'My people will find me most unchanged.'

'Is that true, Iseabail? Do you really believe that?' he smiled, his eyes batting momentarily to my left hand. The hand that had once held my scar. 'It would have been impossible for me to return to my village as a young man,' he said, emotion shining in his eyes. 'Even if I had wanted to.'

I looked at him, perplexed. Did he know that he had touched a nerve? That I had been wondering the exact same thing as I'd stared into the hall mirror yesterday?

'My family back in the countryside would never have accepted the new me – not just how I looked, but how my mind had expanded, opened up to the wonders of the world – you need to think carefully about whether it is wise to return.'

'Then I'll pretend that my life here was no different to that on the island,' I said, swallowing, thrown by my own change of heart. I had intended to return brimming with knowledge but perhaps he had a point: I hadn't thought it through properly. Would the islanders be able to handle the truths about the outside world? The truth about my life at the merchant's house? Even Artair might feel differently about me. What if he worried if I would be satisfied to spend the rest of my life on the island after the luxury to which I had been exposed? What if he knew I had ended up living in the house of the mysterious sailor?

There was a long silence.

'That's quite a pretence to keep up,' said Plaustrell, clearing his throat, 'whilst skinning foul seabirds from dusk till dawn.'

I remained silent, worried his pleasantries were on the wane.

'But please,' he said, raising one hand. 'I didn't invite you here for a lecture. Let us leave thoughts of returning to your island until the time that it matters. Now, didn't I promise to show you atop of that ladder?'

But our conversation had caused me to have second thoughts. 'Maybe I should be getting back,' I mumbled.

The merchant was surprised. 'But aren't you curious?' he said, pointing with a long finger to the rough ladder in the corner, leading up from the mosaic floor to disappear into the ceiling. 'Don't you want to see?'

'I'm worried that the things up there will . . . change me further,' I said quietly.

'I don't make the offer of seeing my workshop every day. Indeed, I may never make it again.'

I mulled over what Maria had said about the wondrous contents of the workshop – about the treasures collected from all over the world. And the fact that I would be allowed to look around properly when she had been shooed out.

Resolutely, I made my way over to the ladder.

Plaustrell put down the tea tray and climbed up first, then beckoned me up through the hole in the ceiling into his strange, wonderful world.

I expected the space up there to be brighter, owing to it being two storeys high and encompassing the remaining windows, but for the most part the room was devoid of natural light. Any that filtered through the panes of grimy glass was blocked by the sheer glut of paraphernalia.

I struggled to take it all in. Rolls of Persian carpet, patterned metal lamps, piles of animal skins, and a gigantic pink seashell were just a few of the things that stood out from the jumble. These were the items sitting in coronas of light emitted from oil lamps dotted about the place, but much more stuff was stacked together in an amorphous mass.

The merchant watched my face as I took in the contents of his room. 'Do you like my collection?' he asked proudly, lighting another oil lamp with a spark from a flint box. The flickering lamp swayed devilishly around the stone walls as he made his way over to the far side of the room. One by one, more objects revealed themselves as he passed.

An eagle dangling in flight, a red fox standing alert, a golden furry beast with its mouth open wide showing spectacular teeth.

'Those animals . . .' I said, pointing at them dumbfounded. 'Are they . . . real?'

'They're real all right,' said Plaustrell, putting the lamp on a table and picking up the fox. The creature stayed quite rigid, its glassy eyes sparkling in the oil light. 'But I think the question that might be more appropriate is . . . are they alive? In which case,' he said, stroking the fox's auburn fur, 'they are not.'

I noticed with horror a monkey sitting on a chair, its glare glassy and unresponsive.

'Don't worry,' he laughed. 'That isn't Nell – she's over there in the cage. That one is stuffed like the rest.'

I observed the cage in the corner, covered by a blanket. 'How can a thing look so alive and yet . . . be quite dead?' I said, turning my attention back to the other animals.

'Come see,' said Plaustrell, holding the creature out to me. 'This fox, for instance – its innards have been removed and replaced with sawdust, its skin treated with alcohol, so that it won't rot. In a way, it will live for ever.'

I stroked the fox but refused to take it from the merchant, its fixed grimace making my flesh crawl. 'And all these other animals . . . they are stuffed too?'

'They are,' said Plaustrell, replacing the fox and taking up an otter which was a more familiar animal to me. 'By my very own hand indeed. A skill learnt from a friend in Rome.'

'What did you do – with their innards?' I enquired.

'What a curious question,' laughed the merchant. 'Most of them were used for meat – what was left for medicines. Some of their organs are highly valued for their healing properties.'

'Goodness,' I said, looking round at the many animals dotted around the place. A nip of dust invaded my nose and I sneezed.

'It's a bit dirty, I'm afraid,' he conceded. 'And rather untidy. But please, step this way. There is more to see!'

The far side of the room was lit more warmly with candles and the piles of stuff petered out to reveal two high wooden benches filled with clusters of pewter pots, mortar and pestles. Above the benches, the stone walls were lined with curved wooden shelves which were jammed with bottles of all shapes and colours. The shelving sat mostly in darkness and I was thankful not to be able to make out the things floating in liquids that Maria had spoken of.

There was also an anvil and a metal fireplace, hung with hammers and tongs and, finally, a writing desk equipped with pots of inks and quills obscured by a tide of yellowed scrolls.

Another pile of objects was hidden by an oriental screen.

'I could do with a bit of help in here,' said Plaustrell walking back over to the stuffed golden creature. 'But I don't like the servants poking around in things they don't understand.'

'What is that animal?' I said, moving over to join him. Up close the creature was huge, wider and even bigger than Whitefoot with paws the size of saucers and a mane of shaggy hair.

'It's a lion,' said Plaustrell. 'I captured him on the plains of Africa. To me, it's the most exciting animal in the entire world . . . the true king of the beasts.'

'And you brought the creature back here . . . and stuffed it?' I said, thinking of all of the representations of the animal that featured in the merchant's house.

'Not quite . . . I caught it alive, took it in a cage back to Venice. Used my workshop there. You can't leave the animals dead too long – the heat makes their hides disintegrate.'

'And its organs are used in medicines?'

'Very much so,' said the merchant, suddenly deep in thought. 'As is its blood.'

I pointed quizzically at an object that I first mistook for a footstool, made from crinkled grey leather.

'An elephant's foot,' I was informed.

'That is a *foot*!' I exclaimed, trying to calculate the size of the beast that could possess such a thing.

'And those are its tusks,' he explained, pointing to two further artefacts by the foot. 'Teeth that stick out from its mouth. It is what ivory is made from.'

I had never thought much about the ivory objects in the house, or the creatures the material might come from. I took a moment to stroke one of the huge tusks.

'Well, I suppose that I should be getting on,' said the merchant. 'And Maria will be missing you by now.'

'But there is so much to see up here,' I began, devastated at the thought of being dismissed. 'Why, I've hardly seen the half of it.'

'I'm flattered by your interest,' said Plaustrell, smiling widely. He picked up the oil lamp again which caught the line of his fine cheekbones, emphasizing the shadow of his beard. 'If you like, you can come back – I'm sure I can think of other diversions for my daughter.' He paused for a moment. 'If you are worried about corrupting that mind of yours – wouldn't you say that the damage is already done?'

'I suppose so,' I said, looking about me. 'I can't exactly un-see any of this now.'

'And why on earth would you want to?'

I looked around at the merchant's treasures – at the

giant urns painted with strange symbols, the skeletons of bird-like creatures, the dusty books stacked precariously.

All this could be at my disposal – all in the absence of Maria.

'I suppose I could tidy up a little.'

'That would be a great start,' smiled the merchant, walking over to the covered cage. 'Though you might also be a useful assistant. And Nell needs looking after too.'

'You mean, help with your work?' I said, fascinated, pulling up the cover to see what Nell was up to. 'Do you think I am capable of such a thing?'

'From what I have seen of you so far, I'd say you were very capable.'

Nell was sleeping soundly at the bottom of her cage.

'She's still getting used to being up in the daytime,' explained Plaustrell. 'After her night-time shifts on the boat.'

'I still can't believe that she helped you sail out all the way to St Kilda,' I said, watching her chest rise and fall.

'Well, it certainly wasn't the easiest of journeys,' said the merchant, gesturing that I should let Nell rest. 'But it was worth it – we returned with the perfect girl.'

'Are you sure about that?' I began, thinking of the silly pearl test on the boat. 'Maria isn't exactly fond of me.'

'She's not used to sharing her things, that's all,' smiled the merchant. 'A result of being kept in isolation – all those terrible tempers and jealousy.'

I nodded in recognition.

'And you have probably noticed her skin flare-ups. My diagnosis is that she harbours an underlying malaise. An imbalance in body humours. Brought on by grief – she still holds tightly to the memory of her mother dying.'

'But I thought that you said that was a long time ago?' I said, recalling that was what the merchant had claimed that night I went to his study. 'I mean, how old was Maria when her mother passed from the plague?'

'It really is time that you left now,' said the merchant, smiling tightly. 'I can't have Maria wandering the estate looking for you . . . And I'll send word of the progress of the supplies, as soon as I have it.'

'That would be wonderful, thank you, sir,' I said, reluctantly moving towards the ladder.

Plaustrell still hadn't mentioned whether he'd informed his daughter about the contents of the scroll he gave to my chief – about the supplies promised to my people, and that I could return home to my island if I so wished. Still, his warnings about returning to my simple life had given me plenty to mull over.

Closing the door, I paused in thought. Unlike Maria, the merchant seemed to think so highly of me – in fact, he thought me so clever and capable that he wanted to involve me in his work. Yet if his potion was successful, Maria claimed he would take his household back to Venice, to this great floating city full of art and beautiful churches, full of treasures far greater than in his mere tower collection. And I wondered if he intended that I go with them. And I wondered . . . if I would like that too?

I studied the carving on the tower door. Now I knew what a lion looked like for real, the outline had more meaning. I could make out the teeth, the fur, the tail that ended in a puff.

And the initials below: AMAP. Alexander Marcus Amanza Plaustrell.

But of course, I said to myself. The son of a poor woodcutter. The boy who had seen too much and could never return to his village.

I shook my head and leant my forehead against the door. I had to return home! No matter how capable the merchant thought I could be as an assistant, I had to return for Artair. This life wasn't mine to live – it wasn't real. What was real was the sea, the island, the cliffs, my mother and my sister – and Artair's arms around me. I closed my eyes and pictured the children we would have, living a life of freedom underneath that endless sky.

But my thoughts were shattered by someone sprinting up the steps behind me: William.

Ignoring my presence, he pushed past me to the door, hammering on it wildly.

'What on earth is the matter?' I said, torn between going back to the house and lingering to know the emergency.

Seconds later the merchant flung open the door and

William made a series of hand gestures before pointing towards the stables.

'Stay there, Iseabail,' Plaustrell ordered, returning into the tower.

William's face was bright red with the exertion and he leant on the doorframe to catch his breath.

'What's happened?' I said, wide-eyed, wondering why I had been asked to stay.

But the merchant was back, a thick silver chain twisted around one arm. 'Hurry now, both of you,' he said, leading the way down the steps. 'We haven't a moment to lose.'

Following William's silent directions, the three of us ran to the woods. Although I hadn't a clue what was going on, the chain brought by the merchant suggested that we were after an animal, one that had escaped.

'Is it a horse we are looking for?' I panted after them, aware of how unfit my current lifestyle had rendered me, but no one replied.

Plaustrell didn't stop until we all entered the trees. Then he halted us, putting one finger to his lips as we caught our breath.

'Listen,' he ordered. But there was nothing. Just the whispering of the trees in the breeze and the squawk of a startled crow.

'It'll be hiding in here somewhere,' said Plaustrell, ushering us forward deeper into the trees. 'Its natural habitat is in forests.'

We walked for a while, the only sound our footsteps crunching on the snowy forest floor. Then Plaustrell stopped dead and held up his hand.

'Look,' he said, pointing to the ground. There was a thin trail through the snow where it had melted. I frowned, remembering the melted snow around the stables. Why was it melted here too? From somewhere near came a faint cooing sound.

I recognized the sound – it was the call of the strange goat!

Plaustrell looked right at me. 'I've brought you along because it trusts you, Iseabail,' he said, looking across to William who shrugged apologetically.

So William had told his master about my visit to the stables and the goat's affection for me.

'But how did it escape its chains? It's only a little goat!' I said.

Plaustrell's mouth twitched. 'It's stronger than it looks,' he said quietly.

'And you think I can capture it?' I went on, not moving an inch. 'Because it licked my hand?'

But Plaustrell was growing impatient. 'Fetch the creature before it strays, Iseabail. I think it is behind that fallen tree.' He handed me the chain. 'The stables are clearly not secure enough any more. We'll have to bring the beast into the tower instead.'

Sure enough, there was a trail where the snow had melted leading up and around a fallen tree. William pointed to a discarded leather hood which was caught on a nearby branch.

I approached alone, feeling strangely light-headed. The closer I drew, the more delirious I felt. Like the time when I'd petted the creature in the stables. I glanced over my shoulder.

Plaustrell watched me in anticipation, his eyes alight with emotion, his mouth twisting unpleasantly. Jealousy? I think he wished he could feel it too.

'Go to it then!' he whispered sharply.

I circled the fallen tree whilst the two men waited where they stood. And there it was, a little bigger than I remembered, cowering beneath the far side of the trunk. Without the hood, a small pinkish horn protruded from its forehead.

My breath caught in my throat as several things ran through my mind at once. I remembered the crate brought on the back of the wagon. Reinforced with bars of iron. And the hood that concealed the creature's head – the marked passage in the compendium of beasts.

A beast stronger than a lion with a horn that can cure any poison. Only tameable by a maiden, pure of heart.

'It's a unicorn,' I heard myself say, though my voice seemed to be thick like it wasn't coming from my own throat, just an echo from the surrounding forest which had shimmered into nothing.

For all my senses were locked on the unicorn, its crying crystal eyes fixed on mine. Before I could reach it, it stood on shaky legs and ran to me. And I placed the chain around its neck.

Later that afternoon, Maria finally shared the *Beast Compendium*.

On any other day, I would have been desperate to see it, immerse myself in those beautifully illustrated texts about mystical beasts. But all I could think of was what had just happened, out in the forest.

'Are you even listening to me? I take the time to read you my book and all you can do is stare into thin air!'

'Sorry, Maria,' I mumbled, trying to focus back on the compendium. She had it open at the page of the aspidochelon, a gigantic turtle often mistaken for an island.

'Well, what do you think of it? Isn't it terrifying?'

'It's probably just a whale,' I said absently, still thinking of the unicorn. 'We used to get huge ones that swam right into the bay. Tell me about the unicorn again. Didn't you say that its natural enemy was the lion?'

At this, Maria snapped.

'I know why you are harping on about the unicorn,' she said angrily. 'I know what happened to your scar!' At this, her hand shot out to grab my wrist. 'Don't think I didn't notice.' Her grip was surprisingly strong, her freezing fingers gripping me tightly like icicles. It had already occurred to me that the creature's lick had completely healed my scar.

'Papa has found his missing ingredient!' she cried out.

'And he's wasting it on you!'

I felt my heart thumping so loud in my chest I thought it would burst through. How much had Maria known all along, really?

But then something else seemed to occur to her, a cruel smile playing on her lips.

'Clever unicorn,' she said, trance-like as I pulled free. 'Now that hand is far prettier without an ugly mark.'

'The creature is not your present, is it?' I said, rubbing my wrist where she'd held it. 'Your gift from your father's travels?'

'The *Beast Compendium* is my present, dear Iseabail. It's something I've wanted for years – the unicorn is just a missing ingredient.'

'The rare ingredient needed in his cure for the plague,' I said dumbly, trying to understand, 'is the unicorn?'

And at this, Maria pulled open the page still marked with the ribbon in the *Beast Compendium*. She turned the book around so that it was the right way up for me. '*A beast stronger than a lion with a horn that can cure any poison,*' she said, without looking down at the book. My eyes fell to the fair-haired maiden and the white beast with its long twisting horn. The creature now locked up in the tower must only be a baby. Did the merchant intend to kill it? To use its tiny horn in his potion?

When I looked back up at Maria, she was staring at a fixed point just below my neck. At the bulge in the silk of my dress, covering up the pearl.

'*Only tameable by a maiden, pure of heart,*' she added with a sly smile before slamming the compendium closed.

'I wasn't brought here to be your companion?' I said, stunned, tugging at the leather twine so that the pearl popped out from my bodice. I felt the anger rising in my chest. 'You believe in the powers of this pearl too. The real reason why I was chosen. You've known about this all along!' I cried out.

Maria bit her top lip, as if wondering how much to give away.

'Well, I don't take kindly to being tricked,' I spat, 'and whatever your father wants from that poor creature, I'll not help take it!'

Suddenly Maria looked bereft. 'Don't say that,' she pleaded, reaching over for my hand. 'Papa was desperate, that's all. He wants to complete his potion so that we can return to Venice. Please, Iseabail, the creature trusts you, you must help us.' She looked up at me, eyes glassy with tears as I snatched my hand away.

'I'm nothing special,' I said. 'The unicorn just likes me because I'm good with animals. This stone – it's just a sea-pearl.'

'No,' said Maria, her voice cracking with emotion. 'No, that's not true.'

'But I still don't understand why he has gone to such lengths to find a cure for the plague?' I said, though I stopped short of bringing up the subject of her dead mother this time.

'If the potion is a success, it will have the ability to heal *anything*,' said Maria, her eyes imploring me. 'So I'll no longer need to take the waters here. I'll be able to go home. To Venice. Don't you understand?'

'And I'll be able to go home too?' I said steadily, though the merchant's warning about returning to the islands invaded my thoughts.

Maria nodded, her eyes fixed on mine. 'After you have helped us with the unicorn, you will be free to return to your island.'

But just then an image flashed into my mind – Mammy, Eilidh and Artair turning away from me, their faces hard as stone. Whatever love Artair used to hold for me in his eyes turned to repulsion. My new self too changed from the island girl they remembered.

'But what if I decided not to return home?' I whispered. 'What if your Papa asked me to Venice instead?'

A ripple of horror crossed over Maria's face. 'My God!' she cried out, her voice rising in hysteria. 'Maybe he does not intend to take me back with him at all?'

I looked at her in confusion.

'If the potion does not work,' she blurted on, 'maybe he will take you back to Venice instead of me!'

'What an awful thing to say, Maria! If he asked me to go back to Venice with the household, we would all leave together. No one is getting left behind.'

I spoke gently now, my own anger forgotten – but Maria would not be consoled.

'I knew it – he's in love with you – with your beautiful skin and teeth. And now he's found out that you are clever too. That you can help him with the unicorn. He must think I'm a lost cause!'

'You mean to say that you really think that your own father would leave you here behind? All alone?'

The wide-eyed look on her face confirmed that she did.

'Maria . . . he wouldn't—' I began.

But her features had become contorted, the red spots rising on her face and neck worse than ever before. 'You mustn't go to him any more!' she screamed. 'I know that you've been sneaking off to his tower! Trying to turn his head. Stay away from my papa!'

I leant over the table in an attempt to comfort her but she picked up a glass paperweight from the table and struck me hard across my temple.

By the time I had recovered myself, Maria had long since run out of the room.

Slightly dazed but furious once more, I followed her up the stairs only to find the door to our shared bed-chamber bolted from the inside.

Even worse, a familiar-looking animal skull was placed outside on the bare floorboards. It was the sheep skull, packed by my mother into the trunk over three months ago.

'Go away, you stinky fish girl,' she shouted at me

through the door. 'Why, when you arrived at this house you smelt rotten – and I wanted to gag!'

'Well, aren't you clever, finding my trunk,' I retorted, banging on the door. 'You had no right to look through my things!'

'I found it because of its repulsive odour!' said Maria, opening the door to sneer at me. Her flecked brown eyes were burning fiercely and two red dots remained, livid, on her cheeks.

'What about you!' I retorted. 'All that awful perfume you wear. Like you're covering up something bad!'

'Well, I've had Sylvia throw your festering trunk away!' she spat, tears welling in her eyes at my insult. 'You should never have brought a thing like that into this house.'

'You threw it away?' The rage drained from me, leaving me weak. Suddenly I remembered how carefully my mother had packed up my belongings and my heart lurched as I thought of how I'd hidden them away, how I'd been ashamed of them. I had been embarrassed by my own people, every last one of them. I felt a pang of guilt as I thought about my handsome, noble Artair. Still on the island, waiting for me. Suddenly I wanted nothing more than to see my trunk again. Be reminded of home.

I tore down the landing and up the tiny staircase, my eyes stinging. Maria was right, I must have smelt rank when I arrived, but the world was a very different place outside of the scrubbed cleanliness of the merchant's house. Peasants like me went about their daily grind without the luxury of soap and hot water! They took on the smells of their labour – fishy seabirds, sweat and animal dung. And that was real life. That was what I had to hold on to.

To my relief, I found the trunk still wedged under the eaves exactly where I had left it – Maria had been lying. Though when I knelt beside it, I realized the fastenings were loose. I sniffed the sealskin, surprised by the lack of strong odours.

I shuddered with emotion as I pulled open the straps, wondering why the smell wasn't more overwhelming, especially as the contents had been shut up there for so long. I wanted to inhale the trapped smells of the island, be reminded of home. Be reminded of who I really was.

Surely the dried puffin had grown gammy by now – and the gannet shoes, well, they always had an atmosphere all of their own. But on opening it, these two items, along with the sheep's skull, were no longer present, and what had been left in there appeared to have been washed. A rough island smock smartly pressed and folded, smelling vaguely of vinegar, the Soay sheepskin neatly rolled reeking of camphor. Any remaining island aromas were emitted only by the trunk itself. This sanitization must have been carried out on my arrival before the trunk was brought upstairs, but I had been too ashamed about my belongings to check on them properly, stuffing them quickly into their hiding place.

'Now the stinky fish girl tries to steal my papa's affections? Well, you can go and sleep with the servants – where you belong!' called the girl's sinister voice behind me. 'Like he'd pick a common thing like you to be my companion if he'd had the choice.'

'Where are the rest of my things?' I demanded. Although I was glad that I hadn't been faced with the things that would rot away, I was furious that they had been disposed of without my consent.

'Gone,' she spat.

But she'd lied to me once already, and I didn't believe her. 'Give me back the skull,' I said, turning to face her. Mammy had been right to pack it – it was the thing that reminded me most of home. There was hundreds of them littered across the islands, picked clean by seabirds and bleached white by extremes of weather. Eilidh and I used to line them up and play a game where we tried to throw seashells into their eye sockets. The memory of two sisters running free as the wind across the clifftops, barefoot, poor and happy, stung like a jellyfish. It was the life that I wished for my own children. 'It does not belong to you.'

'Why do you need it?' she went on, a rash rising in pinpricks across her forehead. 'What use do you have for any of your things right now? Not thinking of running off with the stable boy, are you? Well, wouldn't that be a scandal?'

The girl was making no sense. One moment she was accusing me of seducing her father, the next moment I was eloping with William. *She's sick*, I reminded myself. 'I'll not be running away,' I said, standing up to face her. 'I'll leave this house with dignity. When your papa has arranged my passage home.'

I said this last bit with conviction, my mind still warm with the memories of the island. How could I have ever entertained the thought of going to Venice? I would be going back to marry Artair. Back to my old simple life. Back to who I really was.

Maria's rage faltered. But now she looked faint, dropping down on her knees.

And although I hated her right then, was it really her fault that the merchant had brought me here under false pretences? She was only a child, prone to bouts of rage and weakness, a malaise brought on by the death of her mother.

'Let's just forget our quarrel, shall we?' I said, taking a deep breath. 'I was just angry with you for taking my things, that's all.'

'I've already arranged for you to go sleep with the servants,' Maria said sharply. But her colour was starting to return to normal and I knew the worst was over.

'As you wish,' I said.

She stood unsteadily and staggered back down the corridor into the bedroom, slamming the door closed.

In the kitchens, Sylvia was expecting me.

The beds down there were simple mattresses of straw,

pulled out for the night and stored away in the daytime, but the kitchens at night were pleasantly warm rather than stifling like the rooms above. As I lay down, pulling the rough-spun covers over me, I thought my new sleeping quarters really weren't so bad.

Even so, the events of the day played over and over in my mind as I tried to fall asleep. The unicorn in the forest – its implicit trust in me as I'd slipped the chain around its neck. My discovery of my true purpose here: a girl to tame the unicorn, not a companion to a rich girl. The way Maria's face had contorted with rage as she'd hit me with the paperweight – my temple still throbbed with pain. My trunk, its contents washed of my former life. The endless, bitter argument.

Eventually I fell asleep to the sound of the other servants' snores and I woke at dawn, feeling calm and refreshed and full of purpose. I hoped the kitchens might become my permanent quarters until I left this house for ever – which I intended to do as soon as I possibly could: the very moment the merchant's supplies had reached my home shores.

But that was not to be.

'Good morning, Iseabail,' said the merchant, leading his daughter by the arm into the kitchens, where I was eating my morning meal. 'I do hope that you have slept well.'

'Indeed I have, sir,' I said, cautious. Maria's eyes were fixed on the floor, red as cherries.

'Sylvia came to the tower to inform me of your squabble,' he explained. 'I think my daughter owes you an apology.'

Squabble? Such a trivial word. Did he realize that his daughter had whacked me with a paperweight? I touched my finger to my temple, where the child had struck me. If there was a bruise there, it would be conveniently covered by my hair.

'Maria,' said Plaustrell, his arm draped over his daughter's shoulder. 'What did we discuss?'

'I'm sorry that you had to spend the night down here,' said Maria, though her expression showed none of the remorse of her words. She had not, I notice, apologized for any of her other behaviour.

The merchant looked at me expectantly.

'That's all right,' I said to the child, although I knew now that Maria and I would never recover what friendship we had managed to build. The argument had changed everything.

'Very good. Now that's settled, might I have a word with you, Iseabail?' the merchant added. 'In the library.'

Maria shot me a warning look before being ushered into my vacated seat by Sylvia who fussed and gave her a warm custard tart. She was very pale, and didn't respond in her usual way to Sylvia's attentions, pushing away the tart disconsolately. I trailed behind the merchant to the library.

*

'Maria is convinced that you intend to run away,' he began, urging me to sit on the library's settee whilst he leant casually on the sideboard. The fire was not yet lit for the day and the room was still pleasantly cool. 'Understandably, she is upset.'

I sat on the edge of the settee, my hands steepled in my lap. Had Maria told him that I'd figured out why I was really here? That I was not a companion, but a part of his secret cure?

'And is she upset because she will miss me?' I said, my voice controlled. 'Or that I will no longer be able to help with the unicorn?'

At this the merchant smiled, but the tendons in his neck tightened. 'Does it matter,' he said with false gentleness, 'that you were brought here for a different reason to that which you were expecting?'

He was a devious scoundrel all right, but now I knew that he needed me. Only I could help him tame the unicorn. Surely the power was in my hands now.

'I suppose not,' I said, looking up at him. 'As long as you fulfil the promises that were made in your letter. How are things progressing with the supplies?'

Plaustrell stood up straight and fixed me with a grave expression. 'They reached your island's shores safely.'

'But that's wonderful news!' I said, standing, my heart leaping for joy. I walked to the window, leaning my skirted thighs against the cold sill. Soon, I would leave this place and never think of it again. I took a deep breath and turned to face him with conviction. 'You told me I was here to be a companion to your daughter. You lied. I see no reason for you to keep me in this house. I do not wish to harm the creature you are keeping captive. So, now that you have fulfilled your obligation to my people, I wish to go home.'

'Don't you remember what we discussed?' he said calmly. 'This fantasy of returning to your island – I must warn you, it is foolish.'

'I listened to you in the tower that day, really I did, sir,' I said as genteelly as I could, making my way back across the carpet. 'But all the riches in Venice will not stop me from going home. And my people will accept me back with open arms, I know it!'

'You really think that, don't you, Iseabail?' he sighed whilst resting his hands heavily on his hips. 'And I really didn't want to have to do this. But you have forced my hand.'

I regarded him steadily; what on earth was he up to now?

'I'm afraid I have more news about the delivery of the supplies,' he said, meeting my gaze. But his voice was so grave it made my bravery falter.

'Go on,' I said valiantly. 'Please, I must know.'

'It's your chief,' he said with a sad shake of his head. 'I'm afraid that he is dead.'

'Innes Ferguson is dead!' I cried. At this my legs buckled along with my determination, causing me to sit back down on the settee. 'But how?'

'He fell from the cliffs,' said the merchant. 'I'm so sorry.'

'The cliffs?'

'I believe that is a common death for a man from your islands?'

'Not in winter . . .' I said, wringing my hands which were numb with shock. 'And the chief, why he hardly ever harvested birds any more. Are you sure?'

'Quite sure. And the new chief refused to accept a single box of the supplies on to his shores,' said Plaustrell.

'The new chief?' I said slowly. 'So Artair must have taken his place. But why would he refuse the supplies?' A brief brimming of pride in my chest was replaced by something dreadful. Artair becoming chief could only mean one thing. 'A man cannot rule without a wife on my islands,' I said, dumbfounded.

Plaustrell had by now walked over to sit on the settee beside me. 'That is the tradition of your people?' he said softly. 'That a man cannot rule without being wed?'

'Yes,' I said, with a voice now no more than a whisper. 'Artair . . . he must have married Eilidh.' The betrayal was so physically painful that it felt like a knife in my heart.

'That is your sister?' said the merchant pensively. 'Well, you do not know that for sure.'

'She was the only eligible replacement,' I said. Then I rested my head in my hands in despair. 'That must be why he refused the supplies! They don't want me to come back now!'

The merchant laid a gentle hand on my back as the sobs rose within me.

The decision had been taken out of my hands; I couldn't go home after all. I would be trapped with the merchant and his daughter for ever.

Eventually, Plaustrell left me alone in the library to return to his scrolls in the tower. Latin wasn't until this afternoon and I couldn't just sit among the books, torturing myself about Artair marrying Eilidh – and the meaning behind him rejecting the supplies. Every time I allowed my mind to wander back to the island, it was as if I'd been hit afresh with a boulder in the chest. I dragged myself to the kitchens to offer my services there, but the kitchen maids looked mortified at my gesture of help, Sylvia ushering me out of the room as if I was completely mad.

As another wave of emotion overwhelmed me, I ran to the stables, bereft when William was nowhere to be found. But in all likelihood, I realized, he would be in the tower, tending to the unicorn. I prayed to God that Plaustrell wasn't in there too. How I ached for William's silent, sympathetic company.

I dodged the branches of the sinister tree, its branches sprung up and grabby without the weight of snow, and ran up the steps. I pressed my ear to the door.

The walls to the tower were thick but the door wasn't as substantial. I held my breath to bring complete silence. But after a few minutes of hearing not so much as a scrape of a chair, I concluded that the unicorn must be asleep and neither the merchant nor his stable boy were present in the lower chamber.

But then, as I was about to leave, I heard a male voice. Unmistakably the merchant's.

I put my ear back to the door, picking up the odd word of Gaelic. William must be in there too, maybe gaining more instruction for the care of the unicorn. I wondered when the merchant planned to take the poor thing's horn, hoping that its removal might leave the creature otherwise unharmed. That it might one day be returned to its mother. If only I could see what they were up to.

The clover-leaf window that fed the lower chamber sat a few arm's lengths away from the top step; if I could climb up on the sill, I could peer in.

Inserting my left boot into the groove between two stones, I tested my weight on it. The frost was completely melted on this, the south-facing side of the tower, but the purchase felt slippery, too unstable. Unbuttoning my boot, I kicked it off, attempting it again with bare toes. That felt much better. I followed with my right foot, now also bare and pushed my fingers into the soggy moss in a crack just above my head. I had been brought up to climb cliffs after all – this would be a breeze. Thankfully, I found that my now fuller figure still lifted easily.

Several manoeuvres later, my nose was at the level of the sill. I raised my eyes slowly above the pane and peered inside.

At first, I could not see much, the windows glazed with dirt. Releasing one hand, I wiped away the outside grime with it very slowly to prevent attracting attention. Now I could make out the outline of the room, then figures moving within it.

The merchant was bending over the fireplace doing something with tongs and there was someone sitting in the throne-chair. As I focused in, an unmistakable mop of red hair was poking out above the high-backed seat. I could not see the unicorn and assumed it to be tethered somewhere beneath the window, maybe near the bed where I had fallen asleep, somewhere out of my line of sight.

William's left arm was draped over the arm of the chair, palm up and his shirt sleeve was rolled up to the elbow. What on earth was going on?

Presently the merchant turned around and inserted the end of what looked like a shorn quill into William's arm. William flinched as Plaustrell poked the sharp end into the fold of his elbow.

What was he doing to William? Was he putting some kind of medicine directly into his body? I pulled on my fingers tightly to bring me closer to the window. By the time I looked back up at William, Plaustrell had placed the open neck of a jar beneath the quill, the other end of which was now embedded in William's arm.

Then I watched in horror as I made out a dark liquid move down the transparent stem of the quill. The liquid began to drip into the jar.

The merchant was extracting William's blood.

Although I was shocked by the sight, I steadied myself by recalling Maria talking about the practice of blood-letting in the case of certain ailments, but to my knowledge William was not ill. So why would Plaustrell be extracting his blood?

Eventually, when the jar was a quarter full, Plaustrell extracted the quill from William's arm. The merchant stood tall and raised the glass to the light, swirling the dense liquid around for several seconds, studying its consistency.

After carefully placing a cloth stopper inside the jar, he put it down on a table whilst William wiped his arm. The merchant was going to keep William's blood, but why?

Just then, a piece of moss tore away from the sill below my fingers and I lost my grip. My knees scuffled down the walls before I landed with a thud, barefoot in slushy snow. I crouched there for a moment, worried that the ruckus may have raised attention.

As I feared, there came a jangling in the lock of the tower door. I didn't hang around to see who opened it. Instead I sprinted barefoot off around the side of the tower and fled down the other side of the hillock and hid in a bush.

'Hello?' shouted the merchant in Gaelic. 'Anyone there?'

After several long moments, the door closed again. I waited in the bush for a while, peering up at the north face of the tower. How strange, the snow had melted here too, despite this being the cold, sheltered side. I thought of the slushy trail into the woods and the path up to the stables and knew that it must be because the unicorn was now contained within.

When I was certain the merchant had returned inside the tower, I scrambled back up the slippery hillock to retrieve my boots where I'd kicked them off beneath the window.

Unfortunately, they were no longer there.

I found a pair of woollen slippers back in the house and made it to the library in time for Latin with Father Ronan. But at any moment, I expected Plaustrell to burst in and reprimand me for spying on him.

But I was to find myself quite alone in the library for half an hour. The merchant did not show – neither did

Maria or Father Ronan. At last, Sylvia arrived to tell me – in the slow, stilted Italian I could half understand – that Maria was unwell and had gone to bed. I couldn't help feeling a rush of guilty relief.

But as I stood looking up at the map on the wall, my thoughts about home started to close in on me again, superseding any strangeness I had witnessed in the tower. What should I do, now that returning home seemed out of the question? The thought of staying with Maria in any capacity filled me with dread. Plaustrell was kind enough, and yet . . . Suddenly I was desperate to talk to the priest. Like William and me, he was a stranger here: could he understand what I was going through? Maybe he could advise me?

Father Ronan's quarters were no more than a shabby cell hemmed into the outer wall of the Great Hall. After braying on the thin lattice for several minutes, the door finally opened a crack.

'No tutoring today, Father?' I said, putting one foot in the door so that he could not close it.

'Sorry, no, I'm not feeling the best,' he replied. The priest looked even more dishevelled than usual and his breath stank of malt. My heart sank. He was in no fit state to offer me comfort or advice. Even so, I didn't want to leave.

'I want my lesson,' I pressed on. 'I'm in need of distraction.'

Father Ronan observed the desperate look on my face, then his eyes wandered above my head, searching the Great Hall behind me.

'Maria's not with me – she is unwell. Now please let me in.'

'I suppose you can use my paper and quills,' he said, stumbling backwards into the tiny room.

The room consisted of little more than a pull-out cot-bed suspended on strings from the wall and a desk scattered with inks. A wooden cross hung above the cot and a deep, narrow leaded window afforded ample light to forgo the need for candles in daylight hours. I knew that the priest had been offered grander accommodation next to the chapel upstairs but he had shunned luxury for sequestration.

Father Ronan staggered back to his cot, flopping down on it so heavily I feared the tensed cords attaching it to the wall would snap. He gestured to the chair tucked beneath the desk.

Checking the Great Hall behind me was still empty, I entered, clicking the flimsy door closed behind me.

'Where's the girl?' he said, as I sat on the chair and looked at him forlornly.

'I've already told you,' I said quietly. 'She's not feeling well.'

'Taking one of her baths, is she?' he said, shaking his head. 'Something odd about that girl. Something odd about this whole household.' At this he threw a chunky arm around the room. 'The monastery warned me about the master's obsessions with cleanliness.'

The cleanliness rules certainly didn't extend to his hidey-hole.

'The merchant believes that it can prevent the spread of disease,' I mumbled, though my mind was elsewhere.

'But it is the Almighty that sends pestilence,' he said bitterly. 'A plague can't be stopped by a few bars of soap. And those things that he keeps inside his tower!' At this his bulk gave a visible shudder. 'I snuck in yesterday when you all ran into the wood to catch that goat,' he went on. 'Witnessed for myself his menagerie of death.'

'Those animals are just stuffed,' I said, trying to imagine Father Ronan hauling his bulk up through the ceiling in the tower room. 'Plaustrell told me how he did it with sawdust.'

'Jesus wept,' he went on. 'Now he's got an innocent involved in his debauchery.' But then he noted the look on my face. 'Whatever is wrong, child? I take it you are troubled by something other than the abominations dwelling atop that ladder?'

I nodded my head.

'Tell me,' said Father Ronan, leaning towards me with concerned eyes. 'I am a priest, after all.'

And so I told him about the merchant's promises, the supplies getting through but being turned away. About how I'd never be able to return home. I didn't mention the unicorn. I'm not sure why – perhaps because I thought it didn't matter. What mattered was what I was going to do next.

'And what do you intend to do now?' asked the priest gravely, stroking the week-old whiskers sprouting from his double chin. 'Return to Italy with the master?'

'What other choice do I have?' I said, my voice cracking. 'Am I fated to spend the rest of my days with the merchant and his ungrateful daughter?'

But Father Ronan didn't answer my question: he only barked a laugh. 'Good Lord, the man has everyone fooled.'

'What do you mean?'

'Nobody knows where *that* child came from,' said Father Ronan. But then he hesitated. 'I shouldn't be telling you this. If *he* finds out . . .'

'Please,' I said. 'Don't you think I should know everything if I am to continue to live with them?'

Father Ronan nodded slowly. 'Well, be sure you don't breathe a word of what I'm about to say – to anyone,' he said.

A nod assured him of my discretion.

He took a deep breath of the stale air. 'The first thing you need to know is that Plaustrell's wife died in the last outbreak of the plague in Venice,' he said. 'That was six years ago.'

'But that does not make sense,' I objected. 'For one, Maria has clear memories of her mother dying.'

'Does she now?' said the priest. 'Or is that just a convenient ruse for her to act the way that she does?'

I shook my head, confused. The emotion I had seen from Maria when she talked about her mother's death had seemed real to me. 'And you are quite sure that the outbreak was six years ago?'

'Check the history for yourself!' went on Father Ronan, frustrated at my questioning. 'The sickness killed half of Venice. And I have it on good faith from the abbot at the monastery that he himself read Plaustrell's wife her last rites.'

'If Rachel died in that outbreak, then Maria would have only been a baby. She would be unable to recall memories of her mother's death,' I said, thinking out aloud. 'Maybe it was a more recent outbreak of the disease that took the master's wife?'

The priest shook his head.

'I'm afraid there is another explanation for all this,' sighed Father Ronan sighing deeply. 'The child in this house isn't the merchant's daughter.'

I looked at him wide-eyed.

'She can't be,' he continued sternly, reading my expression as one of disbelief. 'Because the real seven-year-old Maria Plaustrell died with her mother – side by side, on the very same day. I have it on the abbot's authority: he administered last rites to them both!'

I felt a shiver running down my spine, but forced myself to think logically. The priest's story didn't add up. 'Then how do you explain that the girl looks so much like Plaustrell?' I asked desperately.

'There's no denying there's a likeness,' said Father Ronan, cooling a little. 'Maybe it was a cousin he adopted, a child from the same family. Wherever that little devil came from, the merchant's own daughter is dead!'

'But why the deception?' I went on, growing more and more convinced that the priest had it wrong. 'Why pretend that his own daughter is still alive?'

'That's just one of the mysteries surrounding the master,' said Father Ronan, flopping backwards on the bed. Now only the support of his elbows prevented him from completely lying back down, stretching his habit across his stomach like a bloated drum. Then he added, 'I suppose you don't know that he was expelled by the University of Padua?'

'Expelled – as in thrown out? Whatever for?'

'Illegal practices some call *anatomy*,' muttered Father Ronan. 'Not fit for your ears, child.'

I folded my arms, growing tired of the priest's wild tales.

He continued. 'All I know for sure is that I've worked in many a manor and haven't seen anything like it before.' He tipped his head back to stare up at the ceiling. 'It's ungodly.'

'Then why don't you just leave?' I said, peeved he was avoiding my eye. I had poured my heart out to him but all he had voiced was a barrage of strange and ridiculous rumours. 'If, as you say, the household is ungodly?'

'I will,' he said simply. At this, he leant forward and pulled a chipped flagon from under the cot. Then he looked up at me with bloodshot eyes. 'You would be wise to consider coming with me, Iseabail, to Ireland. I would arrange for you to get back home. When the seas are calm again.'

'I've told you!' I said, wondering if he'd listened to a single thing that I'd said. 'I've nothing to go back for!'

'Maybe that's just what the master wants you to believe,' said the priest, lying back down completely on the cot. 'Now if you'll excuse me, I'm in no fit state to teach.'

18

After leaving the priest to his vices, my emotions now in worse tatters than before, I headed for the stairs. I would go and check on Maria.

But my step was heavy as I ascended the wide stairs of the entrance hall, Father Ronan's drunken rant whirling around my mind.

Something odd about that girl, something odd about this whole household.

I liked Father Ronan but the drink had clearly sent him mad. Maybe it was better if he did leave, if he went back home. I was glad that I had not mentioned the unicorn or seeing the master take the blood of the stable boy. Both revelations could only have stoked his delusions.

When I reached the door of our bedchamber, my hand hesitated on the latch. What if Plaustrell had already informed Maria that I was no longer welcome back on my island? That in all probability I'd·be accompanying them both back to Venice?

Surely, she would be furious.

But on entering the room I found myself staring at a neatly made four-poster bed, devoid of an occupant. As further testament to her absence, the fire in the grate had not been lit and Nell's cage had been installed in one corner, though the monkey herself was fast asleep.

I went over to the window sill and looked out across the moor. The sky was unremarkably grey and I could barely make out the posts jutting up through the stilled mist. An image of Father Ronan overriding his pony's fear flashed before my eyes. Now it was the priest who was desperate to escape the merchant's estate.

Before heading back down to the library, I decided to check in the master's bedroom in case the girl was there.

This time, I was met with a wall of heat. The fire was blazing with fragrant pine logs and the room was unbearably hot.

Then I saw Maria, fully dressed, lying on her back on the bed, the lion curtains pulled back.

'Maria?' I said, entering the room. 'Are you all right?'

But the girl didn't respond – she just lay there on her back, eyes shut, the skin of her lids a delicate lilac. I lay my head on her chest and was relieved to feel it rise and fall, but still the girl did not stir. And something felt out of place. Something I could not put my finger on.

Nobody knows where that child came from. The priest's words rang out in my head. Could it be true that Maria wasn't really Plaustrell's daughter? That she was another child adopted to take her place?

But suddenly Sylvia barged into the room. Angrily, she shooed me back out into the dim corridor. After a stiff scolding from her I surmised that Maria was suffering from one of her periods of lethargy and was not to be disturbed.

But the maid refused to leave me on the landing, ushering me down the stairs with a stiff finger-wagging that I was not to go back up there.

It was lighter down in the entrance hall, the afternoon sun spilling dusty rays through the leaded windows, but still I didn't notice the merchant's approach from the library. That is, until something clattered on to the black and white tiles.

'*Torna in cucina*, Sylvia,' said Plaustrell briskly, ordering the maid back to the kitchen whilst I eyed what had been thrown down at my feet. The boots I had abandoned outside the tower.

Plaustrell looked down his nose at me expectantly but thankfully he didn't ask for an explanation.

'I've come to ask for your assistance again, if you would be so kind,' he said instead.

I looked up at him blankly.

'Don't worry, I don't seek your blood,' he said gently, toeing one of the boots with his own. 'Unless, that is, you have had the plague?'

'Sir?'

'That is why I take the boy's blood,' he explained. 'I know what you saw through the window must have looked strange. His fellow villagers cast him out for surviving the plague, believing he must be in league with the Devil when all the time he'd just been born with a natural immunity.'

I looked at him sceptically.

'I believe that his blood contains some of the healing properties I need for my cure. A necessary ingredient I have deciphered from my scrolls.'

'And William does not mind if you take his blood?' I continued, faint with the thought.

'I only take a small amount, nothing his body can't replenish,' answered the merchant.

So Plaustrell had started to assemble his potion – a potion that would cure not only plague, but any sickness, including his daughter's malaise. Their departure to Venice would be imminent – if the cure was effective. I swallowed, feeling sick as I stared down at the tiles of the hall floor. What would I do, since I couldn't go home?

'Maria told me you tried the cure on your wife,' I said slowly, 'but it didn't work.'

'That's right,' said the merchant. 'I had acquired a

whole ounce of a powdered unicorn horn, the central ingredient for that particular potion . . . but unfortunately the batch was not pure.'

My eyes urged him on with his tale though my inner concerns lay only with my own future.

'A charlatan apothecary cut it with an inferior substance,' he went on, his tone bittering, 'and so it did not work.' A shadow passed over the merchant's face. 'But death would not be cheated quite as easily as I'd been.'

Death would not be cheated.

That was the phrase that Maria had used when she claimed she remembered the death of her mother. But Father Ronan had said that the merchant's wife had died six years ago, during the outbreak in Venice. If he was right, the girl's memory could not hold true. But I didn't want to risk asking the merchant about the year his wife had died again. And I didn't want to get Father Ronan in trouble.

'In fact, that is why I require your presence now in the tower, Iseabail,' said the merchant, snapping me out of my thoughts.

'Please – don't make me cut off the unicorn's horn, sir. It's only a baby!' I blurted out.

'And therefore its horn is of no use,' said the merchant genially. 'Too soft until they are fully grown, you see. But it possesses something else of great value.'

He watched the realization dawn on my face; it was the creature's blood he needed my help to extract.

'With this final ingredient, my potion will be complete, and Maria will have no more need to take the waters here.'

'Maria will be completely cured? And taking the blood will not hurt the unicorn?'

'Like taking the boy's,' said the merchant, a reassuring grin spreading across his lips, 'the procedure will bring the creature no harm. And yes, Maria will be entirely better. No more violent outbreaks. No more evil tempers. Well, no more than an ordinary child,' he said, smiling wider.

And once it was done, the household would leave for Venice.

If Maria was better, perhaps we could find a way to be as we were when I had first arrived. And wouldn't I want to look after the unicorn? Perhaps, I thought, gazing up at the tower, perhaps I *could* go with them.

P laustrell instructed that I must take a bath before I came to the tower. Admittedly I'd managed to avoid one for almost a week and one of the servants, most likely Sylvia, must have informed on me.

This time though, I rolled the large barrel used for storing towels in front of the door of the bathhouse so that the interfering servant could not follow me in. I would take a bath, but only on my own terms.

After lowering myself into the fragranced water, I forced my mind to consider a life in Venice as part of the merchant's household. The sooner I came to terms with not returning to the island, the better things would be for everyone. And, although things would always be difficult with Maria after everything she had said and done to me, without her tempers, life would be bearable.

And I would gladly take up the merchant on his request to become his assistant.

The merchant would need me after all, to manage the unicorn. And surely he would be bringing his trusted stable boy along too?

It was difficult not to picture Artair and Eilidh, difficult not to feel angry and sad and betrayed. But I forced myself to look ahead at the life that was now open to me. Would it really be so bad?

I took up the horsehair brush and scrubbed my finger-nails, thinking about William. If we both went to Venice, then maybe . . . just maybe . . . we could have a future together. He might not have a voice, but William had kind eyes, strong shoulders and steady employment. He was gentle too, and sweet. Thinking of how we had laughed together over the 'goat' brought a small smile to my lips. Of course, I was ashamed to be thinking such thoughts so soon after realizing my engagement was over, but clinging on to the memory of Artair had the potential to destroy me. Abruptly the smile fell away. Distraught, I unwound my hair and tugged at it hard before I washed it.

After the bath, I re-dressed in the fresh clothes that had been set out for me. The merchant seemed deter-mined that I should be clean before I helped with the extraction. With my hair still damp, I set off for the gardens and the tower.

But when William opened the door at my knock, I found that he was not similarly cleansed. His face was streaked with sweat and a fresh cut glistened on one cheek. Then I noticed his shirt. Torn so severely that it hung limply from one shoulder.

'What on earth . . . ?' I said, raising my hand to his cut.

But he caught my hand deftly before I reached it, holding it a moment to his warm face. Like an apology for what was to come.

Then he led me into the lower chamber and I was stunned by the state of the place. Every piece of furniture had been smashed. The beautiful octagonal table now lay in splinters beside the fireplace and the throne-chair looked like it had been hurled at the wall. Now it lay on its side, two legs missing and a crack running the length of its elongated back.

'Is that Iseabail?' said a voice from up the ladder.

'Yes, it is me!' I shouted back, my voice reverberating around the circular room.

William put a finger promptly over my lips then pointed to the bed, or what was left of it. The whole canopy had collapsed over the mattress which itself was heavily torn revealing tufts of stuffing, some of which were scattered around the floor like dead mice.

But beneath the fallen canopy, something was stirring.

The ladder twanged as the merchant's feet descended, but my eyes were fixed on the broken bed. Or rather, what was in it.

'Is it under there?' I said, making to move towards the canopy. William, now standing behind me, gripped his arms tightly about my waist and pulled me back.

'Ah, Iseabail,' said the merchant as his tall frame stooped its way down the last rungs. When he reached the bottom of the ladder, he walked around the circumference of the room, away from the bed. 'William, it's better if we stand over here for now. Let Iseabail approach.'

I was disappointed when William released his strong hands from my waist – but he didn't step away from me just yet.

Then, more movement beneath the torn covers.

I felt William holding his warm breath behind my ear and realized that I too was holding mine.

Presently, a small pink horn appeared above the detritus followed by a creamy white fluff and the unicorn's head emerged.

Its tufty beard sat above a shackle encircling its neck which in turn was attached to the thick chain the merchant had brought after it had escaped the stables. The other end of the chain was fixed into a metal ring hammered into the circular wall behind the bed.

The merchant gestured that I should not make any sudden movements and it seemed that as the animal realized where it was, it became agitated, thrashing its head from side to side so that its beard caught in the shackle.

And then the noise began. That mournful lament, a seal pup calling for its mother. The cry was intense, ear-splitting within the confines of the tower. The clover-leaf window behind my head vibrated in its casing.

I fell to my knees and put my hands over my ears. William fell to his too and put a hand on my shoulder.

'Deafening, isn't it?' shouted the merchant above the ruckus.

The unicorn began to thrash about wildly, pulling at the chain, but although further damage was endured by the bed, it was no match for its tethering to the wall.

Even so, I could never have expected such a tiny creature could be so strong and vicious, or its cry so heart-wrenchingly loud.

'How did you manage to catch it?' I said, rising to my feet once the terrible noise had ended. 'In the wild, I mean.'

'I paid an obliging huntsman,' explained the merchant. 'He was instructed to ensnare a fully-grown beast but ended up with a foal instead.'

'It misses its mother,' I said, a lump in my throat. I felt sorry for the poor thing, despite the alarming damage it had inflicted on the merchant's tower. It was frightened, torn away from its natural habitat, all alone here. In a sense, just like me.

The unicorn proceeded to stick its infant horn into the mattress, ripping it further.

'I need you to calm the creature, Iseabail, so that I can

extract its blood.' For the first time, I noticed the slim instrument in Plaustrell's hand – the quill with which he had used on William. I started towards the bed, then hesitated. I had the upper hand, I reminded myself. I had to make sure my future was secure.

'I take it that you have informed Maria that I am to join you in Venice?' I said boldly. 'That you are to take *all* of the household?'

'Of course,' said the merchant. 'A good decision, Iseabail. When everyone is well enough to make the journey, we shall go to Venice. You shall ride proudly at my side. Now, the unicorn?'

I felt the tension in my body release slightly though I had never ridden before. I glanced at William, who nodded, though his face was tight with some worry I could not read. Taking a deep breath, I stepped forward.

Let's just get this over with, shall we?

I edged closer to the wrecked frame of the bed, marvelling that such a small creature had managed to smash to bits heavy oak. The creature immediately took its chances, leaping off the torn mattress towards me – and I fell to the floor in fright. The chain restrained it, but it reached me, just. Collapsing, it placed its head against my thigh, its cry turning into a vibrating purr.

I looked up at the merchant. He was staring intently, frozen to the spot, holding his despicably sharp quill.

But then the inside of the tower began to fade about me. And I wasn't there any more, I was in a forest. It was summer and there were birds calling all about me, I could smell pine needles, feel the soft breeze on my face. I saw a unicorn, drinking from a clear blue lake nearby. It must have been an adult because it was as big as a horse, with a huge twisted horn extending from its forehead. The horn shimmered gloriously with a greenish-pink pearlescence. I felt my legs running over the soft ground to join it. I peered down into the lake, hoping to see our reflections. But I wasn't me any more. Instead, two unicorns stared back from the mirrored lake. I was by far the smallest. And I had the tiniest pink horn protruding from my forehead.

'Hold it still, Iseabail,' said a stern voice, shocking me back into the cold womb of the stone tower.

'But I saw her!' I cried out.

'Saw who?' snapped the merchant. I realized that he was kneeling next to me now, beside the taut chain, ready to insert the quill into the unicorn's rump. 'What did you see, Iseabail?'

'Its mother,' I said, stroking the creature's head. 'For a moment, it was like—' I looked up at William who had taken a step closer to see better.

'Like what?' said the merchant, impatient now.

'Like I was the baby unicorn – recalling a happy memory!'

The unicorn continued to purr and I wondered if it was experiencing my memories, my home. The white beach down in the bay of my village, the soothing crash of the Atlantic on the shore. That last kiss as Artair held me in his arms. Maybe that would be possible, if the two of us were somehow connected.

'Get the jar, William,' said the merchant with a scowl. Once again he seemed jealous of my affinity with the creature. But I didn't care, for despite the vision fading I had never felt more elated.

'We won't take much,' said the merchant, back to the business at hand. 'A few drops will suffice. So, keep it calm, if you will.'

'Please be gentle with it,' I urged, my awareness now focused back on the welfare of the creature. 'Will you let it go when its purpose is served? Maybe return it to its home?'

Plaustrell didn't reply. He chanced a stroke of the animal's rump, then another, but I knew that he wasn't trying to pet it: he wanted to connect with it too.

The unicorn remained docile across my knee, its blue eyes staring up at me, and only me.

Annoyed, Plaustrell took up the sharp end of the quill and positioned it over the rump.

'Not the best place to extract blood from an animal,' he explained tersely. 'But it's probably best that I remain out of sight at the back here.'

William handed him the jar and retreated.

The merchant struck quickly, pushing the sharp end into the unicorn's fur, just above where the back leg joined to the torso. The quill went in first time, the entry point hidden beneath the white fur, but if the unicorn felt anything it didn't show it. Instead it kept on purring, its entire body vibrating.

Eventually liquid moved out along the transparent stem of the quill. But it wasn't dark and viscous like William's blood or the blood of any other animal that I'd seen, but dull turquoise, the colour of seaweed.

'It's green, just how it has been written!' said the merchant excitedly.

The green blood began to drip down into the jar and the animal remained calm. I dipped my forehead to meet its horn, feeling a crackle of static. Like the approach of a storm.

'Now I must not be greedy,' the merchant willed himself, withdrawing the quill skilfully and standing it in the jar so that not a drop of green escaped.

Then he rose to his feet and moved towards the ladder.

'Your duties here are fulfilled for now, Iseabail,' Plaustrell said tautly, his back still turned towards me.

'Not yet,' I pleaded. 'Just a few more—'

'That will be all, Iseabail!'

William stepped out from the shadows and tugged at the back of my dress. Reluctantly, I prised the unicorn's head off my lap and made to stand.

The animal gave off the most awful yelp and sprang immediately to its feet.

'I'll come back,' I whispered, stroking the point where

the quill had once entered its hide – it was still bleeding a little, and I wished I had something to stop it. 'I promise.'

Its eyes stared up at me, crystals of indigo. The creature was afraid again.

'Both of you are to leave now,' ordered the merchant as his head disappeared up into the ceiling. 'Before the creature gets all stirred up again.'

William took me firmly and pulled me out of the tower, not allowing me to look back. He closed the tower door behind us and led me quickly down the steps, his hand warm in mine.

William quickened his steps, leading me into the sunken garden which was now cast with shadows from the setting sun. Here, he threw me a sad look, then dropped my hand and made towards the path that would take him to the stables, assuming I would take the other path to the house.

'Stop!' I shouted after him. 'Please!'

He did as I asked, turning around as I ran to his side.

William reached down to take up my left hand in his own. He turned it palm down, stroking my newly smooth skin.

'You noticed that the unicorn cured my scar?'

William dipped his head, as if ashamed he had betrayed me.

'That's all right,' I said, putting my hand under his chin to lift it. 'You had to tell him. He would've found out anyway.'

But as William raised his eyes, they glazed over milky, almost like they had frozen. Then he gripped his throat with both hands before dropping to his knees.

'My goodness, what is it?' I said, banging my fist on his back frantically as he coughed violently. 'Have you swallowed something?'

The choking passed quickly and I helped him back to his feet.

'Are you all right?' I said, reaching out to touch his neck, but he stopped me, his eyes watery after the fit. This time he caught my hand with the forefinger suspended in mid-air. We both stared at the tip of the finger, which was stained faintly green.

'Unicorn blood,' I began. Then I looked at the print I had left on William's pale neck, an insignificant smudge sitting just above his Adam's apple.

'What have you done?' said a voice, *his* voice. It was barely audible, no more than a croak – but totally unmistakable. William pulled away, his face pale and frightened – as if shocked at the sound.

'The unicorn blood has cured your voice,' I said wonderingly. I think until that moment I had only half believed in its properties. It was nothing short of miraculous.

His eyes rose to meet mine and he gazed at me darkly, taking my hands in his once more. 'Iseabail, you must go,' rasped William. 'The master is not what he seems. You can't trust him.'

I felt a jolt of fear, but shook my head. 'I can't go home. They don't want me there.'

'I am not an educated man, I can neither read nor write,' he said, 'but even I can tell that Plaustrell will do anything in his power to keep you here. You can't trust his stories. Leave. Home, or elsewhere: anywhere is better than here.'

And with that, he pulled away from me, glancing nervously over his shoulder towards the tower – and his master within.

I was left standing there in the dusk with a pounding heart. Father Ronan had told me not to trust Plaustrell's tale about the rejected supplies – and now William had too. Even I had thought the story about the chief falling from the rocks unlikely . . .

Who was I supposed to trust? I wrung my hands nervously, but William's earnest words were the ones that kept ringing in my mind – and now I was too frightened to stay. I would do as he said. I would leave. And to ensure that Plaustrell would let me go, I needed to convince him that he didn't need me at all.

That night, I sat in the window seat of the upper landing, observing the posts on the moor. As the moonlight struck the tips of their sharp pinnacles, they looked like they were lit from within. White-hot, burning prongs of doom. Tonight, I would tell the merchant that I would not be accompanying him to Venice, after all – instead, I would return home as I'd always planned. If he was telling the truth and I was rejected by Artair and Eilidh, so be it: at least I would know the truth. And at least I would be safe.

But if, as Father Ronan and William suspected, he had lied . . . My heart soared at the thought that Artair was back on the island – that his intention to marry me had not wavered since the day I had left in the boat. Now looking up at the twinkling night sky, I felt more than ever that he was still waiting for me. His heart still true.

I looked down as the pearl round my neck caught the rays of the moon. Plaustrell believed that the stone only remained white when the wearer was of pure heart. It was, however, just a sea-pearl – prettier than the ones I had at home, but no more magical. No one could change the colour of it just by pressing it to their skin. But . . . I would use his silly belief to my advantage. Even if Maria was not exactly kind-hearted, or good with animals, perhaps seeing the pearl unchanged against his daughter's skin might be enough to convince Plaustrell she could tame the unicorn herself, once she was cured. That it was best just to let me go.

But I had to pick my moment. All evening the servants had bustled about, discreetly packing up boxes and crates of belongings, ready for the journey to Venice, whilst the merchant remained in his tower, working on the potion. I hoped he would not be angry with William on learning of the return of the stable boy's voice.

Sylvia passed me by on the landing. '*Stai lontana da li!*' she warned, pointing to the merchant's bedroom and I nodded.

'I won't disturb her,' I reassured the maid. 'I'm going to bed soon.' And I pointed towards my own chamber. Satisfied, she left me on the landing, watching clouds scud over the full moon.

The wind had picked up, rattling the windows and dark clouds formed a fluid veil over the silvery disc hanging in the sky. It looked like there was a storm brewing. I made my way to the master's bedchamber.

I opened the door slowly, this time prepared for the wall of heat. The girl was laid out exactly as I'd seen her last. On her back, asleep on the bed. The air was filled with the usual spicy incense.

'Maria,' I whispered loudly, shaking her gently. But once again, she did not wake.

I untied the leather twine of the necklace, realizing that I had not taken it off since Marcus Amanza had given it to me on the boat. A test, he had said, to make sure he had the right kind of girl. The pearl seemed to pull back to my own skin, like a magnet.

Giving it a sharp tug, I held it up by the twine, the flames of the fire gifting it with a soft, orange glow.

Leaning over the girl, I placed the pearl against her neck.

As I'd suspected: the colour of the pearl remained just the same as the girl stirred a little. I stroked her hair which was tangled with sweat. She looked awful, poor thing, her fine cheekbones cast with greenish shadows. I prayed that the merchant's potion was a success, that she could go back to Venice and live a full and happy life. A life, that is, without me. For she could have her father all to herself.

Maria stirred again, muttering something in her sleep.

It was best that I leave her now, but I would show the merchant tonight – show him how . . .

But then I looked back down at the pearl. Although I still held the twine firm against her neck, I could not make out the stone any more. Because the pearl had turned completely black!

I snatched it up, convinced my eyes were being tricked by the dimness but it was true. The pearl was shiny black, its sheen not unlike the purpled feathers of a crow. Now it was away from the girl's skin, its hue shifted again, shimmering dark silver before returning to white.

'Iseabail!' came the gruff voice behind me.

Quickly, I tucked the pearl into the cuff of my sleeve and stepped away from the bed.

It was the merchant; he was standing on the threshold of his bedchamber.

'I gave strict instructions that Maria was not to be disturbed!'

'I'm sorry,' I began. 'I just wanted to check that she was all right.'

Pacified, he approached the bed and looked over her with concern. 'Trying to work your magic on her, were you, like you did on William?' he said, turning to me with a knowing look.

'It was an accident—' I began.

'Don't worry, William has explained the situation. Seems like you are quite the miracle worker!'

'You are not angry, that the boy's voice has returned?'

I said, aghast that I may have made myself even more indispensable to the household now the merchant thought I was capable of performing miracles.

'Why would I be?' he replied. 'Surely it is testament to the power of the creature's blood!'

It was true that Plaustrell did not look angry. In fact, he looked jubilant, his eyes shining with excitement. How I wished I had something heavy at hand to smash that look off his face. After all the deceptions he had piled upon me. Then again, he hadn't been lying about the necklace.

I looked down at the girl and my skin crawled; why had the pearl turned black against her skin? Wasn't she just like me, just an innocent? How could it be that her heart wasn't pure?

'Now if you would be so kind to give Maria her rest, Iseabail.'

I let Plaustrell usher me out of his bedchamber on to the landing. He was still wearing his crumpled work clothes rendering him shabby besides the walnut panelling of the corridor which was lit conker-shiny by the rays of the moon.

'What's wrong?' he asked as he closed the door behind us. 'You seem out of sorts.'

'You lied to me, didn't you?' I blurted out without proper consideration. 'That tale about the rejected supplies. It's not true, is it?' My heart was pounding as I stared at him, daring him to deny it, half hoping I was wrong.

The merchant looked at me wide-eyed. Then he smiled. 'Why did I think for one moment that I could fool Iseabail McCleod?' he said, shaking his head.

'So you admit lying to me?' I asked, staring boldly into the merchant's amber-flecked eyes. 'Why? Why do you keep deceiving me?'

'Simply, I was terrified you would run away before you took the creature's blood,' said the merchant regretfully. 'Everything I've done, I've done for Maria.'

'And what about me? Now she is to get her cure, you will fulfil your promises?'

The merchant smiled and placed his hand on my arm. 'As we speak, a caravel of supplies is being readied for its treacherous voyage,' he said with a tight smile, as if fulfilling his promise had been the greatest inconvenience. 'Set to leave North Berwick tomorrow evening.'

'And can you also confirm that that girl sleeping on your bed is actually your daughter?'

As I said this, my hand flew to my mouth. I could hardly believe that the words had slipped so easily from my lips. I had never believed them, but the pearl turning black had unbalanced me.

A look of genuine hurt passed over the merchant's face and I knew my instincts had been right: Maria *was* his daughter.

'That priest and his tittle-tattle,' he said, pursing his

lips like he was trying to hold back tears.

'I'm so sorry,' I said, chastened by his expression. 'I should not have said such a wicked thing. I don't know why I did. It's just . . . I'm finding it difficult to tell what is true and what is false.'

'I don't blame you,' said the merchant with regret. 'You must be very confused by my actions. But you have almost fulfilled your duties here, so if you like I will arrange for you to go back on my ship to your island, though I fear that at this time of the year it will not be a smooth voyage.'

I gave a sharp nod of the head, grateful that the merchant wasn't livid at the terrible thing I'd said. If he was to agree to let me go home, I needed to swallow down my mutiny.

'If it's all right, I would like that. Thank you for all that you've done . . . all that you've shown me. And the offer to come to Venice. But . . . I'd like to go home now, please,' I said.

'Very well. A message will be sent at first light to inform the captain that he will be taking a passenger along with his supplies.' He went on, 'Only . . . if you would be good enough as to help me with one more thing tonight? Then you will be free to leave my estate tomorrow.'

'Just one more thing. All right,' I said, bowing my head in mingled gratitude and relief. *If this promise is also false*, I thought, *I shall take up Father Ronan on his offer of passage to Ireland.*

'I require you in the chapel tonight – that is where I intend to give Maria her potion. In the presence of God,' said the merchant, brisk again, making towards the stairs. 'Be there at eleven o'clock sharp.'

'Of course,' I conceded, though I had no idea why I had to be present too.

But then he stopped, stooped his tall frame and picked something up off the floor. 'The necklace?' he said, puzzled, and I realized the cord must have slipped out of my sleeve. He held the pearl up to the moonlight and I prayed that it did not show any signs of having embraced another's neck.

Luckily, the pearl glowed with pure, brilliant white.

'Really, Iseabail, you should be more careful,' he said, walking back and handing it to me.

'What is going on out here?' came the dull voice from down the corridor.

'Maria!' said the merchant, snatching his hand away from mine. 'I'll come and attend to you now.'

But the girl emerged from the room, her outline dark against the backdrop of the roaring fire in the merchant's chamber. I couldn't make out her face, but I could guess she was annoyed at finding me with her papa.

'Why were you holding his hand?' she cried out. 'I told you to stay away from my papa!'

'You've misunderstood,' said the merchant, running to her side as she leant on to the wall for support. 'I was just asking Iseabail to go tell Sylvia to prepare your bath.

Tonight's the night, my dear – and tomorrow, you will be better.'

'Oh, Papa, I feel terrible,' said the girl, beginning to cry as Plaustrell led her back to his room.

'Don't worry,' said Plaustrell. 'Everything is in hand – Iseabail, go instruct Sylvia immediately. And make sure you take another bath too!'

I was in no mood for a second dunking that day though once submerged in the fragranced water, I consoled myself that this might be my very last bath. I closed my eyes, exhausted. It had been a very long day.

And tonight, after whatever duty I was expected to perform in the chapel, I would seek out Father Ronan. If being in this house had taught me anything, it was that I couldn't rely on Plaustrell, although I hoped desperately that – just this once – he would be true to his word.

I began to drift into a sleep when Sylvia fussed into the room with towels, muttering something about it being Maria's turn. I hauled myself out and went to find the clothes I had only put on fresh that morning, but they had been removed. Hanging in their place was an exquisite silk robe, rippling shiny, sapphire blue. I had no option but to put it on, though I wondered for what purpose I was to wear such odd clothes.

Sylvia appeared to comb out my hair, after which she helped me on with the robe before leading me up to my bedchamber. She ordered that I wait there while she fetched me some food.

My tummy rumbled loudly. I hadn't eaten all day.

Nell was wide awake now, fiddling with the catch of the door of her cage, which had been placed in the room after Maria had left. I let the creature out and tried to entertain her with a game of dice. But it was obvious that Nell was missing her real master. At one point she jumped up at the door of the bedchamber, almost succeeding in twisting the handle open.

Thankfully, Sylvia appeared with food for us both: some biscuits for Nell and a cup of hot broth for me. The maid urged me to drink it while it was hot, but I was so hungry I didn't need encouragement. I wolfed it down in her presence, wondering what delicious meat it had been broiled from.

But after eating her biscuits too quickly, Nell seemed intent on getting her hands on my broth, trying to pull the flagon out of my hand at every opportunity.

'You are too much of a bother and I must go soon,' I said, knowing that there was only a quarter of an hour before the merchant and Maria were expected in the chapel. The meal seemed to have given me back my strength and I was now desperate to get this whole fiasco over. 'In fact, perhaps I shall go ahead and pray. It would be good to make my peace with God before everyone arrives.'

To the monkey's annoyance, I put her back into her cage.

Once outside the chapel, I clicked the secret latch so that the concealed panel door popped open. Then I knelt on one of the cushions and prepared my beads for prayer.

'Dear God,' I said. 'Thank you for giving William his voice back. Please let the merchant's potion work, so that he can take Maria back to Venice. And please guide me, Lord, let me find my way back home. Amen.'

My eyes were full of tears as I gazed around the extravagant chapel. But I wasn't looking at the richly painted Bible scenes, nor the fine carvings or exquisite tapestries. All that filled my mind was returning to my simple life on the island. The cooling dank of the blackhouse, the genuine love of Artair.

Just then I heard footsteps outside in the corridor.

The panel clicked open and the merchant entered the room. 'Good evening, Iseabail,' he said, regarding my robe favourably before walking past me to the front of the chapel. He crossed himself and knelt on a cushion at the front.

I stood still, listening to him praying quietly in Latin and I noticed he'd placed a glass jar full of brownish-green liquid up on the altar. Was this the potion for Maria? I wondered.

The door clicked open once more and this time it was Maria who entered, guided by Sylvia, who led her up to join the merchant before returning to the corridor. Strangely, Maria was dressed in an identical sapphire robe to mine, her hair still wet from the bath, but her cheeks were puffy and swollen, as if the water had been far too hot even for her.

She forced a smile at me and I returned the gesture, trying not to think about the texture of her skin nor the cloying sweetness of her fragrance as she passed. Poor Maria. She was far sicker than I had imagined. I guess that explained her foul tempers, her paranoia about me and her papa – and maybe even the odours that she took such pains to cover up.

'Sit down here, Maria,' said the merchant, guiding the child to the front pew. 'And Iseabail, please come and join us.'

I did as he asked, though I still wondered why I needed to be there.

I had assumed he had requested my assistance tonight because of another task involving the unicorn, but as far as I knew the creature was still shut up in the tower.

Just then the door clicked open, this time with some force, and Father Ronan barrelled in. 'What's going on here?' he demanded, looking around at the gathering in bemusement.

I was heartened to see that Father Ronan had tidied himself up since the last time I saw him, his habit clean and his gaze sober. Maybe there really was a chance that he could help me to escape, if Plaustrell had been lying once more.

'Papa?' said Maria, desperate-looking now. 'Can we just get on with it?'

Plaustrell glanced up at the jar on the altar, an anxious look on his face. 'Please leave us now, Father,' he said. It seemed to be an effort for him to keep his voice calm. 'This is not church business.'

'Tell me first what blasphemy takes place in this house of God?' said Father Ronan, striding to the front of the chapel. Then seeing Maria, he pointed. 'And what is wrong with that unnatural child?'

At this Maria began to cry.

'Get out!' demanded the merchant, standing in front of his daughter to push Father Ronan away. 'Or you'll regret it.'

Despite the merchant's willowy frame, he was strong. Father Ronan was no match for him.

'Don't worry, I'm leaving this house tonight,' spat Father Ronan, making for the aisle. 'Before whatever is in that tower finally escapes. There's a tempest brewing on the moor. Brought on, no doubt, by whatever evil is afoot.' Then he stopped and turned to look at me. I tried to beg him with my eyes not to leave tonight. To wait until the morning, when I could go with him if I needed to. 'Iseabail, come with me now,' he said. 'Whatever that fiend has promised you, don't believe it. Leave with me while you can.'

At this the merchant completely lost patience. 'Get out!' he screamed, picking up the ornamental silver arm from the altar and throwing it at the priest.

The reliquary whistled past Father Ronan's head, smashing down on to the flagged floor, scattering its dusty contents as the priest stood there incredulous. He seemed more alert than I had ever seen him before, staring at the broken pieces in pure shock. Slowly, he started to gather up the remnants in the pockets of his robe, heedless of Plaustrell's raging.

'That was a genuine relic,' he muttered. 'Just wait until the abbot hears about this – and whatever godless ritual you are about to perform in this holy place.'

But just then, Nell crawled from beneath a pew. I realized with horror that I must have left her cage unlocked.

'Who let that animal in here?' said the merchant, who had gone to the altar to retrieve the jar. Father Ronan was now standing staring at me like he did not know what to do next.

While Plaustrell's back was turned, I mouthed to him: *Wait for me by the tower.*

The priest gave me a covert nod of recognition and my heart sang with relief.

But now Nell was intent on seeing her master. As she

ran and jumped up at him, the glass jar was knocked from his hands.

Miraculously, it didn't smash nor spill its contents, but rolled across the smooth flagstones.

Plaustrell batted away Nell angrily. 'Stupid beast!' he said, scooping up the jar.

But Nell was not to be deterred. This time, as she approached the merchant again, the girl blocked her way. 'Get away from my papa, you filthy ape,' she said, attempting a weak kick at the monkey's head.

Baring her teeth, Nell took a swipe at the girl.

Maria gasped, doubling over. 'That wretched monkey!' she cried out. 'Its awful sharp claws have scratched me!' At this she sat back down on a pew and pulled up the hem of her blue robe.

As I moved closer, I made out three thin lesions scored into her mottled shin. For a second the claw mark pulsed white, the blood forced beneath the surface. But then the colour returned ten-fold and the slits erupted.

'You are bleeding,' began the merchant, putting down the jar on the sideboard again. 'Everyone, stand away, stand back!' Hastily, Plaustrell untucked his white shirt and tore a length from the hem.

'It's just a scratch, isn't it, Papa?' said Maria. 'Nothing serious?'

But the merchant hurried towards Maria with the same urgency as if her jugular had been severed with a sword. Quickly, he tried to cover the wound with the strip of cotton. But all was in vain.

'Look at her blood!' gasped Father Ronan, who was backing away slowly. 'It's—'

'It's just a scratch,' Maria spat. 'The lot of you – stop staring at me!' Furious now, she tried to press the strip of cotton firmly to her leg.

'Why, your blood, Maria . . . it's completely black,' I said, the blood draining from my own face.

In a panic, Maria dropped her bandage. The piece of cotton drifted down to the floor of the chapel, the three gory stripes already hardening to blue-black crusts.

'No wonder you were expelled from Padua,' cried Father Ronan, wide-eyed at the sight of the dark stains. 'Dissection of a live child, the rumours said. More like resurrection of a dead one!'

'Papa!' cried Maria. 'Papa – make him go.'

At this the merchant sprang at the priest and held him by the scruff of his cowl. 'Out,' he said. 'Leave my estate right now, or by God I won't be responsible for my actions.'

But Father Ronan would not be silenced. As the merchant marched him towards the door he cried out: 'Iseabail, take heed! We thought that that fiend must have replaced his dead child with another – but look how he parades around his daughter's corpse instead.'

What is the difference between a body that is living and one that is dead? Movement, I had told Maria. And I was desperately clinging on to that thought as the priest was evicted from the chapel.

But didn't Father Ronan's rantings tally with my own observations? The freezing hands, the skin prone to plague-like sores, and finally, the thing that was amiss when I'd gone to check up on the girl as she slept in her father's chamber. I had put my ear to her chest, noted the rise and fall of her lungs. But now I knew what had felt wrong, what was missing. There had been no heartbeat!

Then there was the pearl. It had turned blue-black. The same colour as Maria's blood.

'Papa.' Maria had begun weeping as welts material-ized on her wet cheeks. 'Papa, what is happening?' But instead of looking like a rash this time, the swellings on her face rose quickly and immediately began to leak yellow.

Just like that dream I'd had of waking in the tower – a living nightmare. *Maria died of the plague, along with her mother. The abbot had performed the last rites himself.*

Could Maria really have been brought back from the dead?

But no, as I listened to the pleas of the child, I still refused to accept the possibility of it all. Maria was just a sick little girl who needed my help. None of what Father Ronan claimed could be true. I clung on to that thought as I clung on to my sanity. *I will not believe it.*

'Quick, we must help her,' I gasped, glancing at the merchant's anguished face. 'Tell me what I can do!'

The merchant looked at me with utter relief. 'Thank you, Iseabail,' he whispered. 'I'll explain everything to you – I promise.'

Plaustrell knelt down beside his daughter, a broken man. He'd tried everything in his power to cure his sick girl of her malaise and now it looked like he finally might lose the battle for her life.

We laid Maria on her back on the flagged floor, her body in shock. She was shaking, wide-eyed with fright, staring up at her father. I felt so sorry for them both.

'Let's get her out of here,' said Plaustrell, not taking his eyes off hers. 'In case that lunatic priest comes back.'

W e got Maria to her bedchamber and locked the door, the merchant insisting that the cold room would be best to calm her skin. Outside, the wind rattled at the window and from some-where in the distance, a crack of thunder.

Thunder, I thought. Thunder in the middle of winter?

Placing Maria on her back, we propped her head up with the pillow. The welts on her face had waned a little and the merchant tipped the mixture into the side of her scabbed mouth as I held it open.

'I'd hoped to do this in the presence of God,' he murmured. 'I thought we could use the help of some greater power.'

'God is everywhere, sir,' I reminded him softly.

At this the merchant looked reassured.

The residue in the jar remained faintly green but strangely left a stain of stark red on Maria's lips.

Maria's chest still heaved softly, like she had fallen asleep. That's all it is, I told myself. Sleep. Maybe her heart was so weak that I had not been able to hear its faint beat last time.

'Now we wait,' said the merchant. 'Why don't you lie down beside her, hold her hand – that way she won't be alone when she awakes.'

'I think that you owe me an explanation for all of this first?' I said, sitting down on the edge of the bed wearily. Despite my fatigue, I did not relish lying down beside Maria, nor touching her icy skin. I was not sure she would want to wake beside me, either.

'But you look quite worn out,' said the merchant sympathetically. 'And I hope that you have at least been fed this evening.'

'Sylvia brought me broth,' I said dismissively. 'But I demand answers before I turn in for the night. No more lies. No more games. The whole truth. Don't you owe me that much?'

'Of course,' said the merchant, sitting down beside me. He took a deep breath. 'It is true that I brought my daughter back from the brink of death,' he began, checking over his shoulder to see that Maria was asleep. 'Cured her using the blood of a unicorn.'

'You have already used a potion containing unicorn blood in the past?'

The merchant nodded. 'Unfortunately, like the alicorn powder I used for my wife, Rachel, the sample was imperfect – just a few dried drops that I'd acquired in desperation.'

'So Rachel died from the plague but Maria did not?'

'It was a miraculous thing that Maria survived – but it was just down to medicine, a successful tincture. Not a macabre resurrection. But I'm afraid the whole thing was witnessed by a jealous contemporary of mine. Let's just say he retold the story to academics at the university in a rather different way.'

'The abbot at the monastery?'

'That's right,' continued the merchant. 'After Rachel's funeral he spread the rumour that Maria had died too, that he'd given them both their last rites.'

'Why on earth would he do that?'

'Because he had always been jealous of my abilities, and longed to ruin my reputation. He wanted to believe that my potion had failed, that I was unable to save my family. He told everyone that I must have buried Maria and replaced her with another child – just to prove that I was brilliant.'

I nodded my head, trying to take it all in.

'But Maria never truly recovered, her life always hanging by a thread. That's the real reason she was brought here to the moor. So the waters could sustain her until I found more unicorn blood.'

The merchant paused.

'I never dreamt I would acquire a live animal. Nor get my hands on fresh blood. But I always clung to the hope. And God answered me. I acquired the unicorn from trading contacts on the continent . . . and then I found you. My final prayer was granted.' At this he stared up at the ceiling, like he was thanking God.

'But why me?' I asked, stifling a yawn. All I wanted to do was sleep but I needed answers first. 'Why did you choose me?'

'I sailed to three islands before yours, Iseabail. None of them could supply what I required. The odds were never in my favour. A literate young girl from an untouched part of the world . . . it was folly. It was fate.' His voice was full of warmth now. Full of kindness.

'But why was it necessary that the girl chosen should be able to read and write?' I said, thinking of how Mammy might have been right to think my literacy a curse. If Father hadn't taught me, then I would never have been taken away.

'Maria insisted on it,' laughed the merchant, shaking his head. 'She said that any being she was to spend time with should have an agility of mind, a fluid dexterity of hand.'

This last part didn't really make sense. So the merchant had rejected other girls that were pure of heart all because they were not literate? All just on a whim of his daughter?

'And you truly believe that the potion will cure her – completely?' I said, struggling to process my thoughts now I was so tired.

The merchant nodded. 'If I have translated that scroll correctly – and I've added the other ingredients in the correct measures – then before morning, my dearest Maria will be quite restored.'

'Just one more question,' I said, mustering my last ounce of energy. 'Father Ronan said that Maria was seven years old when she caught the plague . . . and that the outbreak in Venice was six years ago? But how can that be?'

'That's right, for once the fat monk has got his facts right,' said Plaustrell, bending over to take hold of my legs and hoisting them on to the bed. 'Maria hasn't grown since her last treatment of unicorn blood. My daughter is thirteen years old. Now, if all your questions have been answered, why don't you get some sleep?'

I looked up at him in disbelief as a flash of lightning burst through the lattice glass. But the merchant seemed unconcerned at his incredible revelation about Maria's age. Now he was calmly lighting a candle at the side of my bed and I noticed he'd already lit one to balance in a holder on a stool beside Maria.

'You said yourself that she was very grown up for a seven-year-old,' he laughed, bending over me now and pushing my head gently down to the pillow as thunder rolled above the roof. Then he took my left hand and entwined it in Maria's right. I badly wanted to untwist them and sit back up but all the energy had drained from my being.

'What's that smell?' is all I could mutter as I found the girl's freezing hand coiled around mine. For my nostrils had been filled with a familiar putrid odour I had not smelt for some time. The burning of animal tallow.

I looked into the merchant's eyes as he bent over me again, searching for so many answers. What was the meaning of the blue robes, and why was he burning animal tallow? Didn't he abhor it and claim that it smelt like death itself? But there was no feeling behind those amber orbs of shifting colour. I remembered only how his nose wrinkled up at the rank vapour of the candles and his teeth glinting yellow as another flash of lightning lit up the room.

Then I remembered nothing at all.

When I woke up it was light. And at first I thought that I'd had another nightmare.

But then I sat up and observed my sapphire robes catching the cold light of morning. And the tallow candles, burnt down to their wicks in their holders. Last night had definitely happened, but now the girl was gone from my side.

I looked around in a rising panic. Had Plaustrell come to retrieve her already? Was she cured now? Or had she died in the night, her body taken away?

It was then that I noticed that Nell's cage had also been removed from the corner. In fact, other than the bed and the stools that held the candles, there was no furniture left in the room at all.

I got out of bed, my legs shaky, desperate for a drink. My head was groggy, like it had been on Christmas morning, but last night I had not drunk any wine or alcohol of any kind. The only thing I had consumed was the broth that Sylvia had brought me.

That delicious broth that I couldn't get enough of.

But there was now no jug of water on the sill. Confused, I looked out across the moor. And there they were, a convoy of wagons chiselled into diamonds by the lattice glass, making their way out from the merchant's estate.

The merchant's household was on the move! But what about me? Wasn't I supposed to be going home today too?

Quickly, I ran from my room, only to discover that everything in the upper gallery had gone. The pictures that had adorned the walls, the mirrors, the rugs, the vases. Running down the stairs, I found more of the same. The chequered hall now looked massive and empty, dirty marks where the furniture had once stood.

I ran through the kitchen barefoot, the faint tang of the copper pans still present after the storm, though they were no longer lining the walls.

Through the sunken gardens, up the steps to the tower, my legs too weak to be able to take long strides.

And that's when I saw it. The tree outside of the tower was on its side, its trunk ripped in half and blackened.

It must have been hit by lightning during last night's storm.

Worse than that, there were someone's legs beneath the felled part, a pair of man's boots sticking out from the huge jagged trunk. I recognized the body with a gasp. It was Father Ronan, still clutching a sack of his belongings. I'd told him to wait for me here, and now—

'Father!' I cried, running to where the priest lay buried. But it was useless, of course – the poor man was dead.

It was then that I heard it: the cry of the unicorn.

I spun round as the last of the household's procession trundled into the trees, spoked wheels churning up the dirty, slushy snow. On the rearmost wagon was strapped the huge reinforced cage I had seen on Christmas Eve, though this time it did not contain the wooden crate but instead was wrapped on the outside in a tangle of thick, silver chains.

Whitefoot followed the wagon, circling it, whimpering, and I thought I glimpsed a flash of white fur beneath the matrix of chains; the unicorn was being transported back to Venice.

'Now it will never be set free!' I cried out, my voice strangely shrill in the morning air.

'As if I could let such a precious creature go,' said a voice behind me. I swung round to look at the merchant. He was high up on his horse, all dressed up in his best riding attire, his black pointed boots polished to a high shine.

'You are ready to leave now?' I cried, aghast. 'What about me?' With the priest gone, the merchant's promise was now my only hope. 'You gave your word that you would arrange my transport home on your ship.'

'I promised many things,' said Plaustrell with a strange half-smile.

'You now intend to bring me with you?' I said, trying to read his expression. 'I am to accompany you to Venice?'

'Not exactly . . .'

What did he mean, *not exactly*? I couldn't think straight, it was all too much. And why did I feel so thirsty, never more desperate for a drink of water in my life?

'Where's Maria?' I managed to gasp, my hands encircling my own throat.

At this the merchant shouted for his daughter.

'Here I am, Papa!' came a joyous voice from the direction of the stables. 'All ready to go.'

Maria sounded quite well. Her voice confident and strong. The potion must have worked.

Then Velvet reared out from the stables. As usual, the spirited creature was not happy in her charge. The horse was snorting, biting at the bit, tossing her head this way and that. Was Maria really strong enough to ride her own horse? In response to its mutiny, the girl administered a sharp thwack of her whip to its rump. The horse fell into line.

But as the grey gelding neared, I realized something.

Maria had grown.

At first I thought that the potion had just taken her back to the size she should have been, a normal size for a thirteen-year-old girl, but when I looked again, I fell back in horror.

For the face looking down from Velvet was not Maria's, but my own.

I pulled my hands from where they still encircled my neck, but studying them now, I realized how small they were.

And there were my bare feet, poking out from beneath the blue robe. Adorned with the dainty toes of a seven-year-old child.

'Dear Iseabail,' said the girl on the horse – the girl with my hair, my eyes, my mouth, but with a quite different smile. 'I can't thank you enough for all that you have done. All that you have given me.' I noticed now that she was wearing a riding outfit that Sylvia had recently adjusted for me, in anticipation of my first lesson. That she was wearing my boots.

'Didn't I tell you I'd found the perfect girl, Iseabail McCleod?' laughed the merchant, turning his horse towards the trees. 'You certainly proved to be compatible. And didn't I promise you'd be riding out at my side? See, in a way you are.' He glanced over in triumph at his daughter – at *me*.

'But the cure . . . the potion . . .' My head was spinning. How could this be? Was I trapped in a bizarre dream? A nightmare? I didn't understand what he was trying to say to me.

'It's true that I brought that body you now inhabit back from the dead,' said Plaustrell as I stared up at the girl on the horse as if she was a ghost. 'But that body is rotten. Infected. Only with special healing waters can it keep even a semblance of life. No, my real "cure" was something rather more . . . ambitious. But you don't believe in magic, Iseabail, do you?'

I was struck dumb with disbelief, but he continued anyway.

'And I'm afraid that logic has been your downfall, your weakness. You chose to ignore all the clues – the tales from the drunken priest, the things you witnessed with your very own eyes. You have been blinded by your modern thinking – it would not let you believe that the unbelievable could be true.'

'Then what is the truth – please tell me!' I cried out.

'That there is no cure for the death of a body, Iseabail,' said the merchant, almost with pity. 'So I used the next best thing – I found my daughter's soul a new vessel in which to thrive.'

'No!' I cried out. 'This is all impossible!'

'But it had to be special,' said the merchant, talking over me. 'A pure-hearted girl to tame the unicorn. A literate girl to grant my daughter a new mind as nimble as her old one. And it's perfect, Maria, isn't it? Wouldn't you agree?'

The girl at his side grinned wider, her horse whickering uneasily beneath her. 'Such a perfect body, Iseabail. Such lovely white teeth and smooth skin,' she said, stroking one cheek with the back of her hand with ecstasy. 'I enjoyed dressing you up like a life-size doll. Now thanks to Sylvia's adjustments, I have the perfect wardrobe too.'

I wanted to protest, to cry out, but I couldn't, my throat so dry that barely a noise escaped me. Besides, everything that had been said made sense. All the ghastly pieces fitted finally into place.

'What's the matter?' The girl on the horse pouted. 'Are you thirsty, Iseabail?'

I felt sick with fright.

She laughed cruelly as I spluttered helplessly on the ground. 'Now do you understand why I was so bad-tempered? Why, if you feel like that all the time you can hardly help it!'

'Now, Maria, you are not being gracious to our benefactor,' the merchant chided softly. 'Iseabail, you have set us free, and for that we are eternally grateful. But I'm afraid now you'll have to live within these grounds, if you want to live at all. For only the waters here will sustain you in your current state. Or you may leave, of course, and die. The choice is yours.'

I'll never go home. Never see Artair again. Never. Finally, I found my voice. 'You tricked me,' I cried. I glanced around at the retreating wagons. Father Ronan was dead, but there was one other person I trusted in this place. 'Where's William?'

'He's gone ahead,' said the merchant. 'I've decided to take him back to Venice with me. I told him you were coming along too . . . though I suspect he might find you a little changed.' He smirked.

But I could not take anything else in. Wild with thirst, I had to find water. I tried to stagger away from them, but the girl urged her horse into my path.

'Oh, and you might as well have this,' said the girl, smiling down from her horse. She lifted something tied around her neck and pulled it free.

My pearl. A pearl turned once again as black as coal.

'Call it a parting gift,' she laughed as she threw it down to me. Then she turned her horse to gallop off with the merchant towards the gap in the trees.

Although I was mad with rage and confusion, wanting to run on to the moor, through the gateposts after them, my thirst finally consumed me.

I raced down the steps through the sunken garden, averting my eyes from the splintered tree outside of the tower.

But when I entered the walled enclosure and reached the trough, I was faced by the lion crest carved into the stone just above where the metal pipe emerged.

And the words from the Bible returned to me once again:

It will not lie down till it eat of the prey; and drink the blood of the slain.

The water in the trough wasn't frozen any more; like everything else it had melted with the arrival of the unicorn. But before I could plunge my hands into it, I saw in horror the face staring back at me.

The face of Miss Maria Plaustrell.

Epilogue

I'm on my hands and knees, brushing out the grate in Plaustrell's old bedchamber when I swear I catch a whiff of the exotic incense he used to burn here – oranges and cloves, ghostly aromas of that fateful Christmas returning to haunt me. Pinching my nostrils, I stand up sharply, only to be confronted by the Lion Rampant stamped into the tiles above the fireplace. There is no escaping the merchant, or what he has done to me. And as I trace the outline of the beast set into the clay with my small soot-caked fingers, I choke on the questions that torture me, over and over again.

Where is he now? That wizard, that fiend? And what has become of my body and the wicked child that resides within it? My natural body will now be worn out – close to forty years old, perhaps nearly at the end of its life. Or could it be that, like *this* one, it has remained quite unchanged? For Plaustrell had fed both of us with his potion that night – I had swallowed Sylvia's hot broth all too eagerly. Two girls' bodies intoxicated with fresh unicorn blood, so that the souls that dwelt within them could be swapped. I lower my hand from the tiles, shivering as I recall the moment I stared down horrified into the trough in the sunken garden – and saw a face that was not my own.

So afraid am I still of being confronted with Maria's face, I avoid all mirrors, all reflective surfaces that hold potential for its manifestation. I've learnt to polish glass without looking, to avert my eyes from the pail as I carry water to my duties, even to avoid the gaze of others in case I should see it materialize in the glaze of their curious pupils.

For although I have been taken on as a maid by the handful of families that have moved through the estate since Plaustrell's departure, my presence here has not passed completely without question. The new owners do not stay long, each leaving after only a few years, citing business or urgent matters elsewhere (when, really, it is the merchant's estate itself that drives them away). But I catch them looking sometimes, either with pity or revulsion, at the sickly little maid, the brown-skinned yet pale bloodless child who keeps herself to herself, who hardly eats a thing but has an endless thirst for water, who, as long as they have known her, has never grown an inch. But luckily, I am treated with the obscurity fitting for the lowliest household rank. I can go about my work invisible, largely ignored, enduring back-breaking hours of mopping, fetching and scrubbing, a distraction from my unnatural situation.

And every night in the kitchens, whilst the rest of the servants snore fitfully, I lie quite still on my pallet, relishing the heavenly limbo between consciousness and sleep. For that is when the unicorn comes back to me, its presence announced by a purr reverberating around the blackened stone walls. Then I feel the spark of electricity brush the skin between my eyes, the very spot that had once touched its tiny, pink horn, allowing me to experience its own happy memories.

Now, as I stand by the fireplace in this moment of unexpected peace, it is like it is with me again. My whole being vibrates in ecstasy as the unicorn returns my memories of the islands.

I'm barefoot on the beach, the sky above a blanket of glittering stars, soft shell-white sand pushing up between my toes. And as the waves pound against the jagged rocks of the cliffs and my lungs are infused with sprays of seaweed and salt, my soul and body are once again reunited.

As suddenly and unexpectedly as it arrived, the vision leaves me, and I'm left standing on the cold, sobering hearthstone. But as always, the feeling lingers, stays with me – like the imprint of a kiss to the lips: it never fails to renew my resolve of returning to the islands even though there might not be a person alive that still remembers my name.

I look back up at the lion with resentment. Mammy would be long dead by now, her old age tortured with the uncertainty of what had become of her eldest daughter. And Artair? Eilidh? Would I never know what had become of them?

My hand strays to the necklace sitting below my rough maid's smock. Whenever I'm troubled with thoughts of home I find myself pulling out the pearl, its resounding whiteness a source of comfort. Still good, I tell myself; still pure of heart. Despite the corruption of this body, my soul remains untainted. My people would be proud of me, for every day I try to be kind to others and work hard to fulfil all that is expected of me. But now, looking up at the lion, I think: why? If everyone I loved is now gone, what am I still being good for?

'Iseabail, whatever are you doing?' comes a sharp voice from the doorway. 'Stop your daydreaming, girl, and get on with your duties!' It is the housekeeper, a terrible old nag with no patience for dallying or idleness.

Quickly, I tuck the pearl back into my smock, just as that familiar, terrible thirst creeps up on me again.

'If I catch you slacking off,' she goes on spitefully, 'you'll feel the back of my hand!'

I stoop to pick up my bucket of ashes, ignoring my parched throat. Someday, I must find a way to be free of the mineral water, find my way back home. And if I cannot, then maybe I won't care about keeping the pearl white any more.

Maybe, I will have my revenge.

Glossary

blackhouse – an early nineteenth-century drystone dwelling of the Scottish Highlands and Islands (no one is sure exactly what type of house a sixteenth-century St Kildan would have lived in but they were probably of similar construction).

cleit – a drystone hut, unique to the islands of St Kilda, used to store and dry birds, crops and peat.

eight-day sickness – infantile lockjaw (tetanus) that caused the death of many newborns on St Kilda.

gout – a form of inflammatory arthritis associated (especially in medieval times) with excessive consumption of rich foods.

guga – a gannet chick. Still eaten (more now as a delicacy) in the Outer Hebrides.

Maiden's Rock – legend has it that the young men had to balance on one foot on a rocky outcrop to prove they would make worthy husbands. The actual rocks on St Kilda are called the Mistress Stone and the Lover's Stone.

Soay sheep – a Neolithic type of sheep that still roam wild on St Kilda.

St Kilda – an archipelago formed from the remnants of an extinct volcano ring. The group of islands (Hirta being the main island, the others being Boreray, Dùn and Soay) sit sixty-four kilometres west of the Outer Hebrides. It was the remotest outpost of the British Isles until its inhabitants were evacuated in 1930.

Stac an Armin – the highest sea stack (around 196 metres high) in the British Isles. I have not used it in its correct geographical location and it would have been Stac Levenish (sixty-two metres) that was visible on the journey from the main centre of population on the St Kildan island of Hirta.

tam-o'-shanter – a traditional Scottish woollen flat cap. Its name is derived from a Robert Burns poem of 1790, before which they were simply known as bonnets.

Gaelic pronunciation

(Scottish Gaelic is a Celtic language closely related to modern Irish and Manx)

Eilidh – Ay-lee

Iseabail – Ish-ah-bel

Gaelic translations

caileag ghealchridheach means literally 'white-hearted girl' (*geal* has all kinds of associations with white/bright/pure)

gaoth means 'wind'

Fun facts

The St Kildans used to eat puffins for a snack – just like a packet of crisps!

St Kildan men developed large muscular feet and ankles (with prehensile toes) over time due to constant rock climbing in search of eggs and birds.

The Gaelic for 'Gaelic' is *Gàidhlig*.

Acknowledgements

I'll probably never be brave enough to make the journey to the isolated archipelago of St Kilda, that jagged glut of rocks rising out of the Atlantic like the pinnacles of a lost world. Situated at over sixty kilometres west of the Outer Hebrides, it is Britain's only dual UNESCO World Heritage Site (now in the safeguard of the National Trust for Scotland) and has many claims to fame, including the highest sea cliffs in Britain. Yet many people have never even heard of it and only a handful each year are daring enough to venture there.

The islands are thought to have been inhabited for over 4,000 years but were abandoned to the nesting seabird colonies and ancient breed sheep in the summer of 1930. *The Pure Heart* is set in the later half of the sixteenth century, a period before significant accounts of day-to-day life were recorded for this remote place. I have, therefore, taken a few historical liberties as to how St Kildans might have lived, loved and died. And, in the absence of evidence for the language spoken at that time, I have used modern Scottish Gaelic forms.

Similarly, the approximate datings of great plague outbreaks in Venice interjected within the story do not completely tally with official records, though the disease was ever present across Europe during that century. Finally, I admit to shamelessly stealing the name Alexander Plaustrell from a real Italian merchant listed as living in Cheapside, London in 1456.

I am still in awe that my story of a peasant girl from St Kilda caught the eye of Jazz Bartlett Love, who sieved out my manuscript from the piles of entries for the Times/Chicken House competition 2018. And so my thanks start with her – and extend to the other judges of the competition – Josephine Hayes, the magnanimous Chris Riddell (who presented all the finalists with their very own bespoke drawing), Florentyna Martin, Joe Brindle (whose kind comments had me tearing up), Martin Pope, Zoë Plant and Alex O'Connell.

And I have so much gratitude for the rest of the wonderful chickens too – with special mention to my editor Kesia Lupo (for patiently coaxing me up my first novel learning curve using the carrot method rather than the stick), to Rachel Hickman, Elinor Bagenal and Barry Cunningham (who might just be the most modest, inspirational and barmy man I have ever met. He did, after all, cook me sprouts in September!). I am also indebted to Dr Sharon Arbuthnot for the Gaelic translations. Isn't it handy when a historical linguist (who is based at the University of Cambridge) happens to live on your street?

I also would like to give a shout out to Tease coffee shop in Banchory (for consistently the best lattes in Aberdeenshire) and to the early readers of the story in its pre-competition *Lion and the Unicorn* manifestation. I was completely taken aback: firstly, that you actually read the whole thing and secondly, that you genuinely seemed to like it. Your feedback was uplifting.

So (in kind of the order in which it was read), my most heartfelt thanks to Sean Kelly, Julie Wood, Jules and Fiona Holland, Hazel Kelly, Fiona Thompson, Claire McCabe, Kathryn Ardila, Blair Michelle Whitehurst, Clare Jones, Claire Cohen, my sister Debbie and my mam June. I'm so sorry if I've managed to miss anyone out. Sharing my manuscript was one of the most nerve-wracking things I have ever done but it was my first step towards becoming a published author.

Finally, to my husband Andrew and kids Fara and Innes. I appreciate that you have given me the space and time to write – and put up with endless outings to grave-yards and historical sites from which I draw much of my inspiration.

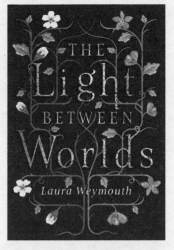

THE LIGHT BETWEEN WORLDS
by Laura Weymouth

How do you live in one world when your heart is somewhere other?

Six years ago in wartime London, two sisters, Evie and Philippa, were transported to a magical realm where they became woodland queens. Now returned to the real world they must come to terms with more ordinary lives.

For Evie, it's unbearable. A patchwork girl, pieced together from pain and longing, she dreams of the whispering trees and a daisy-chain crown.

For Philippa, it's a relief, especially now she's met Jack.

But all it takes are four words to shatter Philippa's new-found peace: Your sister is missing.

As the weeks unfold, Philippa must discover if Evie crossed safely between worlds or if the light was too bright – and she fell.

'Themes of grief, loss and mental health are woven into a cracking story.'
THE TIMES

Paperback, ISBN 978-1-911490-03-6, £7.99 • ebook, ISBN 978-1-911490-68-5, £7.99

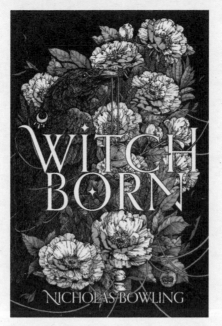

WITCHBORN by Nicholas Bowling

Alyce is in Bedlam asylum – mad, they say. Her mother has been executed for witchcraft, her home destroyed and her spirit crushed . . . so maybe it's true.

Or maybe she isn't as broken as she seems.

A visit from two masked strangers provides an opportunity to escape – and Alyce takes it. Now she must navigate the dark streets of London where there's a secret waiting to be unravelled. In an England divided by rival queens, it seems Alyce has a part to play – if only she can master the rising power within her . . .

'. . . [a] beautifully written Elizabethan fantasy
that crackles with scholarship . . . Nicholas
Bowling is a thrilling writer, who keeps
the reader permanently on edge.'
THE TELEGRAPH

Paperback, ISBN 978-1-911077-25-1, £6.99 • ebook, ISBN 978-1-911077-26-8, £6.99

THE FANDOM by Anna Day

Violet loves *The Gallows Dance* – like every fan, she dreams of being a part of her favourite story.

But the dream becomes a nightmare at Comic-Con, when Violet and her friends are catapulted into the *Gallows Dance* for real. Trapped in a violent, dangerous dystopia, Violet and her friends throw the original plot off course by accidentally killing its hero, Rose.

There's only one way to survive in this world of thorns: Violet must fill Rose's shoes, put the plot back on track, and get out fast.

'Compulsive, intricate and genre-busting:
I am most definitely a fan.'
KIRAN MILLWOOD HARGRAVE

Paperback, ISBN 978-1-910655-67-2, £7.99 • ebook, ISBN 978-1-911077-43-5, £7.99